# GENUS LUPUS

## A NOVEL

by

Julius Charrett-Dykes

Cover art by Julius Charrett-Dykes.

Published in Great Britain by the author.

Copyright © Julius Charrett-Dykes, 2015

www.charrettdykes.com

To

Everyone who encouraged me

I love you for it

(You know who you are.)

ACKNOWLEDGEMENTS

Excerpts from

G. LENOTRE Histoires étranges qui sont arrivées, 1933

Translated and adapted by Julius Charrett-Dykes.

# LA BÊTE DU GEVAUDAN

La Bête du Gevaudan was an unidentified beast that terrorised the northern region of Lozère, France, then known as Gevaudan, between 1764 to 1767. In all, it is known to have killed more than 100 victims, mainly women and children. The beast was described by those who saw it as a rakish, elegant creature often in action on two legs. Surviving victims of its attacks were conscious of a fast-moving brown furred wolf-like animal that could flatten itself to the ground almost to invisibility.

As the beast's attacks intensified, regional authorities organised military groups to hunt it down. When they failed the King of France sent a famous wolf hunter called Denneval and several crack marksmen to track and kill the beast, without success.

In September 1765 a large wolf was captured by Denneval's replacement, Antoine de Beauterre. The attacks stopped, but soon began again, until a certain Jean Chastel shot another large wolf in 1767. However, this wolf, even at an enormous one hundred and nine pounds, has never been accepted as la Bête.

This celebrated spate of attacks was not isolated. An identically described creature had killed over 100 women and children at Benais, nearly a century before. And forty years later at least 21 children and adolescents were killed in the Vivarias region by a similar beast.

Odd savagings and killings by wolf-like beasts have continued in this wild and remote region of France until as recently as 1954.

August 24

The man wrestled the car up the switchbacks that cut a sinewy path up through the green canopy of oaks that enveloped the steep mountainside. As he came around the last corner he swore, the same German registered car was parked on the verge where he preferred to park. He pulled in close behind it, just to make it difficult for it to get out.

"You f*cking Boshes have parked in my space!" he growled, as he switched off the ignition and grabbed his fishing gear from the passenger seat.

He passed by the little pea-green dome tent, pitched in a sheltered clearing about one hundred metres from the road. Grey and black lacy underwear was hanging from the washing line, despite the imminent onset of light drizzly rain. He passed quietly by, catching a glimpse of the golden head of someone in the entrance to the tent, and made his way to the river.

*A* woman looking after a herd of oxen was attacked by a fierce animal. When they saw it, her dogs cowered and ran away. Her oxen grouped together around their keeper and kept the animal at bay.

*Unhurt, the woman came back to Langogne, deeply distressed, her dress and blouse in rags. Because of the fantastic description she made of the monster that had assaulted her, it was assumed that extreme fear had unbalanced the poor creature.*

*It was only a wolf - maybe a rabid wolf - said the sceptic.*

## August 25

The fishing was always good in the gorge, worth the long walk along the difficult path. He'd fished there several times with his brother-in-law. It wouldn't be the same alone, the place gave him the creeps, probably because it felt so claustrophobic when the slit of sky above the river clouded over and the gorge was plunged into green half-light.

Normally he'd have set off before dawn, but he'd breakfasted with the family - much to his wife's delight - and intended to return to the rented gîte mid-afternoon. If he had his brother-in-law Alain along they could bolster each other's machismo, being alone a small fear trembled in the pit of his stomach.

The fear was with him yesterday, but he'd had a good day, catching three decent sized fish. He'd been proud to hoist them aloft on his return, to be greeted as a homecoming hero by his wife Julie and the girls. He'd forgotten the germ of fear that had risen steadily during the day that had forced him to hurry along the rocky path looking back over his shoulder at some danger that never materialised.

Now, it twisted within him: irrational, a product no doubt of the folk-tales that he'd heard from the locals, "You wouldn't catch me fishing there." they'd said. They'd not said why, perhaps because they knew the fishing was good and they wanted to keep it to themselves. Perhaps, there weren't normally fish to found in this part of the river. Perhaps, they knew better places than the gorge. Never mind what they say he thought; he and Alain had taken good fish there, it was worth the walk. The fear subsided a little. He thought of the blonde girl he'd glimpsed in the tent as he passed on the pathway to fish, the watery sunlight on her naked shoulders, oblivious of her pendulous and perfect breasts as she lay on her stomach reading, absorbed and unaware of his eyes upon her. Perfect breasts, the skin honey and smooth, the nipples pink and conical, maybe he'd see them again even if covered by the grey and black brassiere that hung upon the washing line.

Had he imagined the danger that seemed to stalk him yesterday then? That sense of foreboding that had quickened his pace from walk to trot to run? That had found him shaking with relief when the path had at last reached the road and the sanctuary of the car, away from the tent, the girl, her perfect breasts and the grey and black underwear unseeing? The fear lurched and grew within him.

* * *

The grey Golf was still there, but as he pulled up he noticed that a window glass was smashed, so he parked away from it. He also saw that the driver's door was ajar and that papers and pages were strewn in the grass and undergrowth nearby. He walked briskly to the camp, noticing that the papers through which he walked seemed like official travel documents. However, at the camp all seemed peaceful, the sexy undies were still prominent, and everything was as well ordered as yesterday.

He called out, "Hello there!"

No reply...He called again, "Hello!" Still no reply...

He moved closer to the tent, "Hello."

Now he stood right against it and tugged at a guy rope, "Hello! Don't be scared, I've just come to say that I think that someone has broken into your car!" The camp remained eerily silent; he returned to his own car and picked up his mobile phone.

* * *

When Maury arrived on the scene, local gendarmes were already interviewing the fisherman. The sergeant noticed the arrival of the thickset man with old-fashioned thick-rimmed glasses and saluted, "Inspector Maury?"

"Yes," said Maury, "What have you got for me?" he asked the sergeant, a tall blond man in his late twenties who wore his forage cap rakishly

9

and graced his uniform beautifully.

"A vehicle break-in and two missing tourists." the sergeant replied.

"Show me. I suppose I ought to take a look while I'm here."

They passed by the Golf and made their way to the camp-site through slender oaks while the sergeant filled him in, "The fisherman is a regular visitor, comes every year from Bourges with his family for the summer break. Says he found the car broken into this morning and couldn't raise anyone at the camp.

"The Golf is registered in Dortmund to a young student called Fabienne Sonnester." He handed Maury a fax page, on it was a picture of a very attractive blonde girl.

"She is on holiday with her boyfriend," the sergeant continued, "an Italian - Fausto Claudi - also a student at Dortmund." He passed Maury another fax page, the image here of a dark handsome youth. "They could be walking in the mountain. No sign of anything at the camp, everything very ship-shape and tidy."

By now they had reached the camp and the Inspector saw for himself that it looked well-cared for, with plastic dishes washed, washing on the line, a little battery-powered fridge buzzing, the bed made and nothing seemingly out of place. The Inspector raised his collar against the soft, persistent drizzle.

"If they're not back by evening put out a Missing Persons." Maury voiced a hunch, "See what you can find out about the car. Go to the Colonie de Vacances in the village and see if anyone there knows anything." he directed.

* * *

The phone rang at dinner, Maury tutted, put down his soup spoon, wiped his mouth on a serviette, and then listened to the sergeant's report, "No sign of these German kids yet. I'm just putting out a Missing Persons, could be they got lost on the mountain."

"Could be." agreed the inspector, noticing his wife's disapproving look from the table.

"We're sending out search teams in the morning."

The inspector turned his back to the table, "Good. What else?"

The sergeant chuckled, "You were right about the Vacation Colony. A couple of lads there admit to breaking into the Golf and taking a bottle of schnapps and a carton of cigarettes. Say they thought it had broken down as it hasn't moved for days."

"Thank you sergeant, good night." Maury returned to the table.

"Your soup will be cold," observed his wife, sourly.

*A* *few weeks later, a rumour spread in the upper Allier valley that the Beast had re-appeared.*

*In Saint-Etienne-de-Ludgares, on July 3rd, it devoured a 14 year old maiden.*

*On August 8th, it attacked a girl of Puy-Laurent and tore her apart.*

*Later in August three 15-year-old boys from Chaylar-l'Evêque, a woman from Arzenc, a little girl from Thorts and a shepherd from Chaudeyrac were found dead in open country; their bodies terribly mutilated and barely recognizable*

## August 26

Maury hated superstition - it was something he had tried and failed to understand. Here in Lozère it seemed to leech into every part of his world. The dark landscape with its brooding woods and mountains seemed to attract the credulous to join a native people who leaned by tradition to an irrational reverence of the little-known and mysterious. He loathed it because it wasn't built on logic. Logic was at the root of being a detective, logic was based on something substantial, based on fact and evidence, logic was Maury.

His wife's religion was another superstition, every Sunday she uttered her prayers like talismans that would ward off some unseen evil - him - his evil, his unbelief, or rather his open-mindedness. What was her faith based upon? Was it logical? Once, he admitted, once it made no difference, he, Maury, couldn't have cared less - for he loved her. But even love needs to be built on fact and evidence. And the fact was that their marriage, like Lozère, was a dark landscape. Now the children had left there was no sunshine, no glimmer of hope. Their marriage was of habit, of economic logic and of superstition.

That, he figured, was the really galling core of superstition - its failure to look at things as they really are.

Superstition met him at the table, the rituals over spilled salt, the fish on a Friday: It met him in the living room where the television or radio could pollute the home with unclean thoughts: It met him in his work where every new crime somehow had the potential to be committed by a fantastical beast woven by centuries of hearsay, elaboration and, over-archingly, boredom into the Sum of All Fears.

Superstition, to him, denied man his own wonder, his own potential and his own nature. "I am a policeman. I ask questions. Superstitions and religions give me imposed answers. They do not satisfy me. I will keep asking the questions. I am a policeman."

"I am your husband. I ask questions. Your religion supplies you with an imposed answer. You do not satisfy me. Look to me. I am your husband."

I am a policeman. I ask questions.

\* \* \*

He woke with a start and switched on the bedside lamp. The clock said two. His wife stirred grumpily and pulled covers over herself as he dialled the gendarmerie's number and held the receiver to his ear.

"Inspector Maury here...No, nothing urgent, just a message for sergeant Gadret. Ask him to re-interview the boys at the Colonie de Vacances in Rieutort. Ask him to ascertain over how many days the boys saw the German Golf on the side of the road. Ask him to report to me at the German's camp at about eleven tomorrow morning... No, that's all. Thank you, Good Night."

He placed the receiver back in its cradle and switched out the light. He nudged his wife in her ribs, she turned back onto her side and the snoring stopped.

\* \* \*

The Golf was being loaded onto a transporter, a section of gendarmes, clad in shiny waterproofs, scoured the dripping undergrowth in search of clues. Gadret was waiting by the tent that was being dismantled and closely examined by a forensic team. He noticed his superior arrive, bleary-eyed and poorly shaved.

"Good morning inspector, I got your message and I re-interviewed the boys at the Colony this morning..." the sergeant was drowned out by the roar of a dark blue helicopter flying slowly, low over the mountainside.

Maury fished a crumpled handkerchief from his pocket and wiped his nose, "What did the boys at the Colonie de Vacances have to say about the car?"

Gadret got out a leather-bound notebook; "They said they'd seen it in exactly the same spot for four days, so they thought it may have been

14

abandoned."

"Why were they on this road?"

"They say they are seeing some Dutch girls in Laubert."

"The next village on? That's a fair way."

"Yes Sir, sixteen kilometres."

"How did they make the journey?"

"By moped."

Maury smiled and nodded, "How many times did they pass?"

"Twice per evening over the last week, once when going to see the girls and then as they made their way back to Rieutort."

"Does their story check out?"

Gadret shrugged, "I was going to Laubert to check it out in a minute."

"Give me the details and I'll go sergeant," said Maury, "you keep an eye on things here."

Gadret nodded, wrote on a clean page from his notebook, tore it out and passed it to the Inspector.

"I'll call you later." Said Maury.

* * *

Laubert wasn't far as the crow flies, but the mountain roads were a challenging drive. Arriving at the village Maury was eager for refreshment. He found the seedy looking bar in the middle of the slate-roofed village. The bar was empty, but for the 'patron' who was polishing glasses and placing them on shelves. Maury flashed his ID.

"I'm looking for two Dutch girls." He pointed to a bottle on the bar," And I'll have a Ricard please."

The owner poured a generous pastis into the bottom of a tall glass and pushed it over. The inspector dug out Gadret's page from the bottom of his coat pocket.

"Perhaps you know these girls, first names Estelle and Mathilde, they're probably about sixteen, courting a couple of boys from the Colonie de Vacances in Rieutort."

The patron nodded, "Ah yes, I know those girls, only they're Belgian not Dutch. They're staying with a family up the road. Do you want ice?"

"No, just water please."

* * *

"Allo?" To Maury's surprise Gadret's voice was very clear; most mobiles got a distorted signal in the mountains.

"Allo. Maury speaking. Any news yet sergeant?" He could hear that the quality of the call from the phone box was inferior to his colleague's mobile.

"No. The helicopter has gone to refuel and the search teams haven't found anything. Did you track down the girls?"

"Yes, but they were Belgian not Dutch."

"Ah?"

A sticker near the handset of a glamorous semi-clad girl caught the inspector's eye.

Gadret laughed, "What's their story?"

"Same as the boys."

"Do you want the boys charged with breaking and entering?"

Maury hesitated, "No...just caution them. Send one of your burly rugby men to put the fear of God into them."

"Yes Sir."

All he could see beyond the gaudy sticker in the streets of the village were a couple of mangy dogs lolling lazily in the gutters. "How are the girl's parents?"

"Lejeune has got them booked into the Hotel in St. Amans. They're near a phone should anything happen."

"Good."

Maury could hear someone speak in the background. "Hang on Sir," said Gadret, "one of the forensics men has passed me something...they report that they don't think the camp was used last night, it looks like the German couple left it in good order sometime yesterday, probably to go off walking or something."

"How do they reckon that?" He asked as he tore the sticker from the windowpane.

"Discharge rate of the battery on the fridge, assuming it was fully charged when installed on site. And samples taken from their crockery tell us when they last ate."

"That tallies with everything else we've got," confirmed Maury, "Good work sergeant. I'll be back at the station in Mende should you have any news."

Maury tore up the sticker and dropped the pieces into a waste bin as he returned to his car.

* * *

Maury bumped into captain Deschamps in the echoing, tile-floored corridor.

"Ah! Just the man. How are you Deschamps?" he asked the dapper Internal Investigator.

"Very well inspector, thank you." The captain replied, obviously pleased to be engaged in conversation, "How is your attachment to the gendarmerie going?"

"Very quiet, I've been seconded to Missing Persons for the time being." Maury hopped from foot to foot, as he found he did when addressing superior officers.

Deschamps laughed, "Never mind Maury, you could've been seconded to Internal Affairs with me!" he turned as if to leave.

"I'm working with one of your old subordinates at the moment," Maury said.

"Ah yes? Who?"

"Sergeant Gadret."

"Gadret? He's a good man Inspector. You can rely on him." Deschamps put a finger to his nose and dropped his voice to a conspiring whisper, "He was undercover for Intelligence in Marseilles by all accounts, infiltrating a drugs cartel. Got his cover blown and had to be moved out here!"

"Thanks Deschamps."

"My pleasure inspector...has this latest case of yours got anything to do with the missing persons in Pradelles last month?"

"Pradelles?"

"That's right. The gendarmerie at le Puy has been dealing with it."

"Who do I speak to?"

"Try lieutenant Bertillon."

"I will. Thanks Deschamps."

"Not at all." Said the captain, raising his hand as he turned away.

* * *

Maury contacted Bertillon and the le Puy based investigator gave him a précis of the disappearance he was investigating.

A local man disappeared while out fishing at a nearby reservoir known as the Lac du Boucher. His family raised the alarm when he failed to return as he said he would. Police found his car parked at the dam. The man's fishing gear was found at the reservoir side, with live fish in the keep net and his personal belongings in his shelter, including mobile phone, money and papers. It was almost as if he'd just left suddenly and abandoned everything. Divers and search teams, despite exhaustive searches, found nothing.

The man, Alain Descartes, was well known and liked, an administrator in the Mairie, aged fifty-three, happily married with grown up children. There was no history of depression or mental illness, and the man had no obvious enemies. In short Bertillon's team had drawn a blank - there was no suggestion of foul play, therefore the case was still open but regarded as minimum priority. After all, the man might quite simply have walked out of what was undoubtedly a secure, routine and boring life.

* * *

Gadret pulled his exhausted gendarmes off the mountain as the light began to fail. The helicopter banked overhead, a rank smell of unburned fuel in its down-wash, and headed back to its base. Only the local mountain rescue team remained unaccounted for, but such men were quite at home in this rugged landscape. Just the same, Gadret dismissed his team of gendarmes and decided to wait alone to see the rescue team back. Besides, he thought, a glimpse of the stars now that the overcast had broken would be a welcome sight.

Eventually eight dark figures detached themselves from the gloom.

"Anything?" Gadret asked.

The team leader, an unshaven, burly man stepped from the file, "We found these," he said, pulling a brand new pair of trainers from his rucksack, "Found them about one and a half kilometres up the path. One of our blokes went for a crap behind a tree and there they were! Tried to contact you, but our bloody radio's on the blink!"

In the car, Gadret examined the trainers under the interior light:

19

Adidas, size 37 in white with pink detailing, obviously a feminine design. He picked up his mobile phone and dialled.

"Hello Lejeune, Gadret here. Could you ask the family what shoes Fabienne prefers wearing and what size? Tell them it's so we can identify her tracks. Yes, we've finished here for now. You're doing a good job Lejeune, thanks."

"Is inspector Maury still around?" Gadret asked the desk sergeant.

The overweight man didn't even look up from his portable television, "Yeah, he's in his office."

Gadret climbed the creaky staircase and knocked on Maury's door.

"Come," a voice called.

He entered the wood-lined office and put the polythene bag containing the trainers on the inspector's desk. "We found these!" he said.

The inspector looked up from the pile of papers over which he pored and removed his glasses. "Think they're the girl's?" asked Maury, poking the bag with his pen.

"They could be. I had Lejeune ring the parents in Germany. They're on their way here, by the way. According to them she wears Adidas trainers this size."

Maury polished his spectacle lenses with a yellow duster he took from an open desk drawer. "Where were they found?"

Gadret explained. Maury sat back in his chair, replaced his glasses on the bridge of his reddish nose, looked up and nodded. "Take them to forensics and get the duty team to look at them," he directed.

"Yes Sir. Anything else?" asked Gadret.

Maury loosened his tie and undid his top button, "Grab us both a coffee and come back."

* * *

Maury spread the map out on the desk. "Right, the camp-site is here," he said, jabbing at a point on a little departmental road. "Laubert is here, to the east, nine kilometres as the crow flies, in the next valley...

"Here is Rieutort, seven point five kilometres to the west. And here is where the trainers were found - fifteen hundred metres to the north."

"Towards the gorge," pointed out Gadret.

"Yes, that's right. And there are no other roads in the area."

"Except for a forestry track running about a kilometre away, just here," said Gadret pointing out an indistinct line.

The myopic detective leaned over for a closer look, "Right, put a team out there tomorrow, look for anything unusual. Any idea if there are any forestry operations going on up there at the moment?"

Gadret shook his head.

"I'll find out," said Maury writing himself a reminder on a desktop pad. He turned back to the map, his brow furrowed, "Why would she take her shoes off?" he asked aloud.

"Well, they are new. Maybe they were hurting her feet." Guessed Gadret.

"How far would she get with bare feet?"

Gadret considered, "Not far, the path is pretty stony."

"So tomorrow we need to have a good look in the area they were found."

*I*n September, a girl from Rocles, a man from Choisniet, a woman from Apcher all disappeared; what little could be found of their mortal remains were found scattered in open country.

On October 8th, a young man from Pouget returned home, terrified, half dead: he met the Beast in an orchard and it slashed his scalp and his chest.

Two days later, the forehead of a 13-year-old child was slashed and his scalp ripped off.

On October 19th, a 20-year-old maiden was found horribly torn to pieces around Saint-Alban: the Beast savaged her, drank her blood, and ate her entrails.

August 27

He was tracing his finger along the carved images of the apostles. His finger stopped on the chest of a small brow-furrowed figure.

"Who is this Papa?" he asked the priest changing candles at the high altar.

The priest came over, put on thick spectacles and looked over the boy's shoulder at the figure. "That son is Thomas Didymus, the Twin, sometimes known as Doubting Thomas. See his puzzled expression?"

The boy nodded, "Is that why he is frowning?"

The priest chuckled, sat down on the front pew and beckoned his son to sit with him. The boy complied and listened attentively as his father spoke, watching the eyes brighten in the handsome bearded face.

"Some people think that doubt is a bad thing, that true faith is blind. You see, Thomas was told that Christ was raised from the dead after being crucified and entombed for three days by John and Peter, who actually saw Jesus outside the tomb. And by some other men who claimed to have walked and talked with Him on the road to Emmaus. So, while the remaining eight disciples seemed to have accepted their word, Thomas would only believe in Christ's resurrection if he saw it for himself..."

The boy interrupted, "But there were twelve Apostles Papa. You said John, Peter and Eight others. With Thomas that makes eleven."

His father's mouth tightened, "Yes son. But Judas, who had betrayed him, had by this time hanged himself."

The boy nodded understanding and the priest continued, "Well, Jesus then appeared to all the disciples. Poor old Thomas could still barely believe that he was seeing his dead friend and Master alive again. So Jesus held out his hands so that Thomas could see where the nails that secured him to the cross had been driven in. Then he invited Thomas to check the wounds in his side and his feet too."

23

"Did Thomas believe then?" asked the boy.

The priest smiled, "Yes he did, and I think his faith was made all the stronger for it."

"So it's alright to doubt?"

There was a long pause, as his father weighed his words, "We should not believe things blindly. We should always seek evidence.

"Not only that son, we should be prepared to look for evidence where others do not. Some say that faith is blind; I think that is wholly untrue. Faith opens ours eyes and allows us to see what others do not. Some say you cannot see God, I think that too is untrue. God can be seen everywhere if we look for him diligently.

"Always seek Truth son – weigh all the evidence. Rule nothing in, rule nothing out..."

Gadret remembered his father's words and they had become his mantra.

Rule nothing in, rule nothing out.

* * *

Maury arrived at the gendarmerie at six and noticed that the minibuses and vans had already disappeared from the compound.

"Has sergeant Gadret already got the search teams together?" he asked the Duty Officer.

The man nodded, "Yes Sir. They left about forty-five minutes ago. Gadret left you this." He passed Maury a memo that detailed the planned search.

"Thanks," said Maury, yawning widely. "Pardon me."

He rang Gadret when he reached the office, "Bonjour Gadret, you made an early start!"

"Yes Sir, I wanted to make the most of daylight. We've just arrived at the camp-site and we'll soon be off along the path towards the gorge. Another team are coming at us from the forestry track; they say that it looks pretty overgrown, so it will probably take them a while to get to us."

"Does it look as if any forestry is going on?" Asked Maury.

"Well, the team have been told to look for anything that indicates recent activity. If they report anything I'll get back to you." Gadret assured him.

"Okay Sergeant, I might be over to see you later."

"Alright inspector, see you later."

Maury replaced the receiver. Just then the fax machine whirred and spewed out a forensic report. Maury pored over it. "Merde!" he muttered.

* * *

The inspector was met by the duty gendarme in the hotel lobby. The uniformed officer was conspicuous in the Art Deco interior. "Show me to the Sonnester's room would you." Maury directed.

The gendarme led Maury up a large spiral staircase, with a well-worn bannister curling upwards on ornately decorated wrought iron. The treads creaked as they mounted and alighted on a plushly carpeted landing. The uniformed officer knocked discreetly upon a heavy six-panel door, opened it and stepped aside for Maury to pass.

Entering the apartment, Maury found the Sonnesters cradling one another in a corner of the large leather sofa. The missing girl's red-eyed parents looked toward Maury anxiously, they had obviously not slept, they held tightly to one another and looked at him in both fear and hope.

"Tell me a little about Fabienne please," said Maury, settling into a chair opposite.

Frau Sonnester reached out to photo on the coffee table in front of them and turned it, it was a full-sized copy of the one Maury had seen previously, an airbrushed soft-focus portrait.

"A beautiful girl." Maury conceded.

"She is studying at University in Dortmund," Frau Sonnester said proudly, stiffening her back, "She wants to become a doctor."

"Does she live at home with you?" Maury asked.

"No," Frau Sonnester looked sadly at her husband's drawn face, "She has a place with her boyfriend Fausto."

"Have they been together long?"

"About a year."

"Fourteen months," Herr Sonnester interrupted, "She moved in with him in November last year."

"Do they get along well?"

The Sonnesters looked at one another and nodded. "Yes, they do," affirmed Fabienne's father.

"Do they argue?"

"Everyone argues," said the father defensively.

Maury sat silent looking at their faces.

"They've had a bad patch recently," Herr Sonnester unwillingly conceded, "But they're alright now." His voice cracked and he looked downward. "It was just a bad patch. We all have bad patches."

Maury nodded slowly. "But they've put this bad patch behind them...Tell me, has there ever been anything more than argument between them?"

Both shook their heads, their eyes looking puzzled.

"I'll come straight to it Herr and Frau Sonnester." said Maury, not willing to prolong their agony. "Last night one of the search teams found Fabienne's shoes and we passed them on for forensic examination. The laboratory found minute traces of blood on them; there were two types..."

Frau Sonnester buried her face in her hands and her head collapsed into her husband's chest. Maury continued, "One type matched Fabienne's and the other matched her boyfriend Fausto's. In itself this evidence is inconclusive, but to be frank it's bad news...I'm sorry!"

Herr Sonnester cradled his wife and rocked back and forth, both had shrunk deep into themselves.

"I'll keep you informed," said Maury.

"Thank you Inspector," croaked Herr Sonnester.

* * *

On the pathway to the gorge, the forensics man showed Gadret the evidence;

"This rain doesn't make our job any easier," the scientific officer complained.

"Here," he said pointing at the path "is where we think someone was attacked." He indicated faint marks in the grass, "The victim was dragged to behind those boulders."

He pointed uphill and led Gadret up the steep bank to the rocky outcrop overlooking the track. Around the outcrop, white overalled forensics people were down on their knees in the scrubby undergrowth. "We found bloodstains on the rocks here, and just over there by those trees is where the girl's trainers were found."

"Anything else?" queried Gadret, sensing that the man had more revelations.

The man's eyes glittered triumphantly behind his droplet-covered glasses as he held up some small specimen bags. "Some hair," he said, "and this little earring!"

Gadret took the bags and examined them; in one were a few strands of golden hair, in the other the jewellery. The earring was quite distinctive, a small gold dolphin with a tiny diamond as its eye.

* * *

"We are appealing to anyone who has been in the area around Montjaux and Amplaing in the last ten days. We are particularly interested in speaking to anyone who may have seen or spoken to either Fabienne or Fausto."

Maury hated cameras; he looked uncomfortable as he spoke, and his clothes were conspicuously outmoded and worn under the glare of the lamps.

The svelte interviewer at his side now took over, "Thank you inspector. That was inspector Maury who is attached to the gendarmerie in Mende. He is leading this investigation into the disappearance of the pretty young German student and her Italian boyfriend while camping here in the rural idyll of Lozère. A disappearance that is becoming more and more like a murder investigation as police teams uncover sinister evidence..."

Maury detached his microphone and passed it to a technician. As the television reporter continued with his sensationalising, he walked over to Gadret and his waiting car.

* * *

The sergeant drove towards Mende.

"Well sergeant," said Maury, polishing his lenses, "it looks like we've got a mystery to solve. The commissioner agreed to let me have you on the investigating team, so it looks like you'll be out of uniform for a while."

Gadret remained silent, his intense green eyes concentrated on the road ahead, but eventually he spoke, "Who else is on the investigation?"

"You and I are the team," grunted Maury.

* * *

"Okay, so the earring is definitely the girl's. The hair samples come from the girl. The other samples were what then?" asked Maury.

The inspector paced back and forth looking out at the wet grey roofs of the town and the flight of pigeons that wheeled through the chimneys.

Gadret looked through the complex report, "Wildlife. Squirrels and badgers, by the look of it, plus some unknowns."

The men fell into a pensive silence, Maury crossing to the window so that he could watch the people scampering through the rain into brightly lit shops in the town centre below, while Gadret continued his study of the papers on the desk.

"Maybe the boyfriend killed her," ventured Gadret.

Maury crossed to the desk and began casually perusing the Italian's file.

"Maybe. We've only found a few of his bloodstains, and they were on the girl's shoes. But somehow I doubt it."

"They are arguing on the path," Gadret reasoned, pushing himself back in the chair to stretch his long legs under the desk. "They fight, the girl fights back and he ends up injuring her badly. He drags her into the undergrowth and finishes her off there...

"No, you're right, it doesn't figure," Gadret conceded, "Who would pull a body up a hill rather than down the slope? Besides he doesn't look that strong in his photos. Not only would he have to pull her up the slope, but also to carry her off somewhere to get rid of her body!"

"No," agreed Maury, closing the file, "It doesn't look like it was the boyfriend. I suspect that he's dead too. So where the hell are their bodies?"

Once again the investigators lapsed into silence, until Maury now sat restlessly flicking through the pile of papers, admitted his thinking.

"I can't help feeling that our case and Bertillon's are connected," he admitted. At Gadret's puzzled look he explained the case of the fisherman at Pradelles.

"But that is over eighty kilometres away!" Gadret observed.

"Nonetheless, I think that it may be worthwhile to visit le Puy and see what they've got."

*T*he whole county of Gevaudan was quaking in fear.

*A Captain of the Dragoons called Duhamel, made himself available to lead a troop to hunt down the mysterious animal.*

*When Duhamel surrounded and killed an extremely large wolf there was a short-lived period of relief.*

*But this ordinary wolf was not the Beast; the Beast was alive, well and wreaking havoc elsewhere.*

August 28

He watched the scenery slide by as they travelled north. The car climbed into cloud and descended into rain as it traversed the granite slopes. There was little to see, occasional stone buildings planted here and there in the bleak landscape.

White blobs were sheep in the fields. Black stains were vast plantations of windblown conifers in the valleys. The route nationale bypassed remote villages with shiny slate roofs, closed shops and ramshackle industrial areas.

When he'd arrived in Lozère, its otherworldliness had been an attraction, but that had been a good summer, the cool nights and breezes had been a relief after the swelter of his native Roussillon.

But then, she had been the real attraction, the smiling and attentive local girl, he'd met at the Leisure Centre. He'd then accepted a post in the provincial backwater of Mende and foregone a more illustrious career in order to marry and raise their family in safety and security.

Now the children had gone, the smiling and attentive local girl had become stuck in her ways, as sour, remote and infertile as Lozère.

On the approach to le Puy Gadret shook Maury from his reverie, "We're nearly there Sir."

* * *

At the gendarmerie Bertillon met the two officers from Mende and greeted them warmly. He led them to his well-appointed office, handed Gadret a buff file and showed him how to access the computer database.

Then he suggested that the sergeant work in peace while he took Maury off to meet the other detectives based at the station.

In the quiet of the office, Gadret spread the papers out in front of him, and accessed the database files on the Pradelles case.

In actual fact Bertillon seemed to be working on three disappearances.

Gadret accessed the dossiers of these others just to see if they had a similar profile. He saw that they were both young women. The first, a young unmarried mother who had taken up jogging in order to regain her figure. She had failed to return from an early morning jog in a suburb of le Puy. The other, a fourteen year old who left her parents a note to say she was sorry to break the rules but her friend's party, at a nightclub in the centre of Yssingeaux, was more important than her school work. She never made the party.

The ex-boyfriend was the main suspect in the first case, a well-known ex-offender, out from prison on licence, the other.

* * *

"Well, did anything catch your eye?" Asked Maury as they drove back towards Mende.

The inspector smelled of spirits, the officers at le Puy had obviously been very hospitable, and he seemed sleepy.

"Nothing. It looks to me as if the man simply fell into the reservoir and drowned," replied the ever-alert sergeant, flicking the indicator stalk.

"Mmm," murmured Maury, dozing off as Gadret gunned the big Peugeot's powerful engine and sped the car past some labouring lorries.

*I*n October, a peasant from Julianges, called Jean-Pierre Pourcher, was stowing some bundles in his barn. Dusk was falling on the snow covered countryside. Suddenly, a dark shadow passed the narrow window. Gripped by a 'kind of terror' that he could not later explain, Pourcher took his shotgun, stationed himself in front of the stable's dormer and looked into the village street to see a monstrous animal, such as he had never seen.

*'It is the Beast, it is the Beast!' he said to himself.*

*Although Pourcher was courageous, he was shaking so much he could barely hold his weapon. However, after piously crossing himself, he shouldered his rifle, aimed and fired.*

*The Beast fell, and then got straight back onto its feet. It shook its head, as if to clear it, then stood still and looked around trying to locate its attacker. Maintaining his composure Pourcher reloaded and fired again: the Beast howled, went down onto its haunches and with a long leap escaped headlong through the village making "a noise like two persons breaking up after a dispute".*

*That night, Pourcher was convinced that, but for a divine miracle, all the inhabitants of Gevaudan were doomed to be eaten.*

August 29

Inevitably there is order, even behind seeming chaos. An organised pattern behind the random. Stars birth and die sending debris into space that collides and consolidates into matter to eventually form another star. The Universe had a beginning a point of origin where the event that formed it occurred. Behind the smattering of stars that paint the cosmos, perpetually moving, perpetually expanding and contracting, is order.

Sanchez enjoyed patterns; they were his life's work. An enigma was simply to be analysed until the lines could be drawn across un-numbered dots and the picture revealed — it just took patience and time.

Time he reflected, is something he had lots of and too little of.

He picked up the phone.

* * *

The desk sergeant passed Gadret a memo as he arrived at the gendarmerie; he looked at the message and picked up the desk phone.

He listened to the inspector's sombre answer-phone message and spoke after the beep, "Hello inspector. Gadret here, just letting you know that I'm following a lead. I am with a certain Professor of History, Dr Gerard Sanchez, 14 Rue Victor Hugo. He says he can give us clues to help us solve our case."

* * *

Sanchez opened the door to Gadret and motioned him into the apartment, "Thank you for coming sergeant."

Gadret was acutely aware that his raincoat was dripping water onto the immaculate parquet floor, but Sanchez seemed not to notice. The flat was full of books, their musty smell permeating the gloomy interior. The professor was wizened, wearing a pink fez, a gold dressing gown and with his black-waxed moustache he looked a little like

Groucho Marx. He led the sergeant through a corridor lined with books, into the drawing room.

"You've no doubt heard of the Bête du Gevaudan?" queried the Professor, Gadret nodded.

"I think that she has returned!" Sanchez exclaimed.

"I see," said Gadret cautiously. "And what makes you think that a beast killed the students?"

The Professor winked and touched the side of his nose before pulling a large scrapbook from a shelf.

"I have been following strange events in the region for a number of years. Just as a hobby you understand. As you know the Bête is an enigma, but undoubtedly a fact. Well, there has been a pattern of attacks over the last few years - unsolved disappearances, sightings of strange animals - all within a clearly defined geographic area."

He explained as laid the scrapbook carefully on the table and tapped it with his finger, "All the evidence is here. Proof that the Bête is still here among us!"

* * *

Don't tell me," said Maury, as Gadret sat into a chair on the other side of his desk, "this Sanchez has a Bête theory?"

Gadret nodded and slid Sanchez' scrapbook onto the desk, "Quite persuasive this professor, a very brilliant man."

"There's a beast theory for every disappearance or murder in this area," Maury growled, "They all sound convincing, but there's no mythical beast roaming the countryside. They're all romantics, even this professor Sanchez. With all his brains and qualifications you'd think he'd know better!"

"Maybe," said Gadret.

Maury raised his eyebrows, "You think it's worth considering then?"

36

From his lap Gadret pushed two forensic reports to the inspector. "The first is from our own investigation, the other is from Bertillon's. Note any similarities?"

Maury began scanning the reports carefully. "Look at the list of 'unknowns' on both," Gadret hinted.

Maury looked at one then the other, his brow furrowed until he found the commonality. "Yellow-grey animal hairs were found at the site of both incidents."

Gadret nodded, "I managed to get them double-checked," he said.

Maury looked up expectantly.

"They are wolf hairs!"

"You don't honestly believe these people were taken by wolves do you?" Maury asked incredulously.

"There's only one way to find out," said Gadret, "We'll have to see the experts at the Marvejols Wolf Park. They'll be able to tell us what sort of wolf these hairs come from and whether it could be a man-eater."

* * *

Gadret looked from the window at the grey wolves amongst grey rocks under grey sky. To him the animals simply looked like large lean dogs, but their eyes betrayed their savage nature, unblinking and yellow they saw and measured everything.

Maury stood near the attractive young woman at the microscope.

"These are the hairs of a grey wolf," confirmed the zoologist, looking up from the instrument with serious grey eyes.

"What can you tell us about grey wolves Doctor Platigny?" Maury asked, looking at the cups and rosettes for fell running that lined a shelf and the photographs of Platigny clad in running clothes. Her fitness for her sport would explain her spare frame and slightly hollowed cheeks, the inspector thought.

With her eyes Platigny indicated the animals in the high-fenced compound visible beyond Gadret, "Most of the wolves here are grey. They grow to about two metres, they hunt in packs and avoid man at all cost."

"Are they man-eaters?"

The doctor shook her head, "No. Definitely not!"

Gadret turned from the window. "Have any of your wolves ever escaped?" he asked.

Platigny looked uncomfortable, "Yes," she admitted.

"How many?"

"We've had a few incidents."

"How many wolves involved?"

"None at all this year. Last year we lost eight when a tree came down and crushed the fence."

"What happened to those?"

"We managed to monitor them pretty well until they started going north-west from here. There the terrain is more rugged and the farmers are not tolerant. There are still regular sightings."

"How many wolves do you think are left out there?" asked Maury.

"All eight."

"If eight wolves got together could they kill a person?"

"Maybe, it is possible, but highly unlikely. It would have to be a child, a woman or a sick person. But only if the wolves have no choice."

"What do you mean?"

"I mean that wolves have only ever been known to attack and eat man when there is nothing else on the menu. Say, like in Napoleon's retreat in Russia, in the dead of winter, when even the wolves are desperate and starving, and everyone is too weak to fight the wolves off. But here there is plenty of natural prey for a wolf, especially at this time of year."

"Why would we find wolf hairs in the area of two disappearances?"

"It is probably coincidence."

"Even if the incidents were eighty kilometres apart?"

* * *

"We need to take another look on the mountain," said Maury, "The wolf hairs could be a red herring. Maybe we are missing something; my gut feeling is that we have to look at this being a human affair. But this investigation won't go far without more concrete evidence."

"Is it worthwhile getting Doctor Platigny to take a look?" asked Gadret.

"Maybe, if we don't get any more leads."

"What about Professor Sanchez' theory?"

"That scrapbook of his contains cuttings from local newspapers and journals, there is nothing we don't already know in it," Maury looked across at Gadret as he dismissed Sanchez and saw the sergeant's jaw tighten.

"I got this from the German police today." Maury pushed a printout toward the sergeant. "Fabienne was remarkably well-off for a student, she had nearly four thousand Euros in her bank account at the end of the academic year."

"Meaning what?" queried Gadret, "perhaps she worked or her parents provided for her."

Maury shook his head. "Fabienne had no independent income and her parents did not support her."

"The boyfriend then?"

"He is well-off." Maury admitted, "But if you look here..." he pointed at the list of transactions, "you will see that Fabienne was credited five thousand Euros twice in the past three months. She paid off her overdraft and rent arrears with the first payment and made her bank account healthy with the second."

"I see them." said Gadret, "The Credits are from a company called Eurorevenue, it sounds legitimate."

"The payments are legitimate." Maury affirmed sadly.

Gadret shrugged, his look quizzical "But?"

"Eurorevenue make extreme pornographic films."

"A lead then?" Asked Gadret.

"We'll see." Said Maury returning the paper to the pile in his pending tray.

*S*uch tales spread terror; isolated fields were abandoned, streets deserted; people never went out alone or unarmed.

Meanwhile, Captain Duhamel and his troop of Dragoons were making daily beats; 1200 peasants, armed with shotguns, scythes, spears, and sticks escorted them. As soon as the Beast reappeared, they would hunt it down. Criers brought out the peasants in all villages; the braver men got organized and scoured the snow-blown country roads, resolutely hunting the monster.

August 30

Skeletons in the closet, we all have them, mused Maury.

So the pretty German student managed to pay off her debts by getting involved in pornography. A legitimate business in Germany perhaps, but from experience Maury knew the majority of pornographers to be at best seedy, and at worst out-and -out criminals. The sex industry has slaves, pimps, addicts, victims and abusers behind its glossy facade.

For now though, Fabienne's skeleton could remain in the closet. Dortmund was far away – this lead could remain, for now, in his pending tray.

It was still raining outside, Maury went to his locker and changed into cagoule and wellington boots.

* * *

Light drizzle swirled about the four men dressed in foul-weather gear.

Gadret and Maury walked cautiously ahead of the uniformed gendarmes, on the treacherously slippery path to the gorge from where the students camped. Soon they reached the site where the evidence had so far been gathered.

"This is an ideal spot to make an ambush," remarked Gadret looking at the rocky area on the right, overlooking a point where the path narrowed. To the left the ground fell away to a ravine.

"Did we check the ravine?" asked Maury, his thick glasses practically opaque with droplets and vapour.

"As far as possible. There's a torrent at the bottom of the cliff and rocks downstream," Gadret replied.

"What's upstream?"

"White water and a waterfall, then it goes through the gorge itself."

"Was it checked?"

"As far as the waterfall."

Maury looked around carefully. "Let's check the ravine again," he ordered.

It was a difficult descent. The place was green with moss and the white torrent roared over rocks and boulders, and Maury had to shout to get his instructions heard. Then carefully Maury and one of the uniformed gendarmes travelled upstream on the right, while Gadret and the other followed a parallel course on the other bank.

Between them the torrent rushed over rounded rocks or slowed in deep green stretches where the silver backs of large fish flashed. Several times the men slipped on the treacherous rocks but soon they could hear the booming of the waterfall echoing through the narrows.

Maury was overtaken by his younger, more sure-footed companion, who went on ahead. Progress became impossible for Gadret and his companion who came against a sheer face, at the foot of which the water boiled as if in a cauldron.

When the shrill sound of a whistle pierced the roar of the water, Gadret and his companion quickly retraced their steps to a place where they could ford the water on stepping-stones and scrabbled towards the waterfall on Maury's bank.

The three men arrived together at the foot of the falls to find the fourth gendarme. He pointed to the foot of the cascade, it was hard to make out, but there among the stones sticking through the white froth was stretched a pale human hand.

* * *

The body lay on a stainless steel table bathed in bright light. The coroner's breath came out in mist on the cold air, the smell of decay was rank.

Both wrapped in overcoats, Maury and Gadret listened to the coroner's informal report, "We have a positive identification from Herr

43

Sonnester, it is Fausto Claudi their daughter's boyfriend."

The coroner looked down at his clipboard, "The body has a combination of injuries which include a fractured skull and a broken left forearm and lacerations to his neck, back, hands, under forearms and shoulders and torn ligaments in the right angle."

"Did these wounds kill him?" asked Maury.

The coroner shook his head, "The blood loss certainly contributed, but he died of exposure, probably due to the cold and intense shock."

"Can you piece together his last moments?"

"It would be conjecture."

"I would like to hear your theory."

"It looks to me like he was attacked by something with multiple sharp curved claws or blades. Whatever attacked him was going for his throat but he managed to protect himself by raising his arms and this deflected the slashes to his neck and shoulders. I think he must then have fallen from the pathway into the ravine on his back; he tried to break the fall and sustained the injuries to his forearm. However, he fell head first fracturing his skull and causing a cerebral bleed and compression. He was being driven by adrenalin, even with such severe injuries he managed to reach the falls, though he twisted his ankle very severely. He must have thought that he could hide in behind the waterfall, but a combination of the cold water and his blood loss killed him quite rapidly."

"In short then he was running for his life?"

The coroner nodded, "Yes, I'd say that he feared that whoever or whatever had attacked him would continue to pursue and kill him, so he tried to hide. The amount of adrenalin in his blood was enormous."

"One last question Doctor," said Maury. "What attacked him; an animal or a man?"

The coroner shrugged, "I don't know."

* * *

Outside the morgue Maury drew a breath, "We need to interview the fisherman who reported the students missing."

"Is he a suspect?" asked Gadret.

"There were big fish in the ravine..."

Gadret extracted his notebook "Daniel Abrages from Bourges, staying in a Gîte in Rieutort." He copied the details onto another page and ripping it out passed it to Maury.

"You're off tomorrow aren't you Sergeant?"

"Yes Sir, unless you need me."

"No, I can deal with this." said Maury slipping the page into his pocket.

*T*he hunter's quarry eventually reappeared near the Chateau de Baume.

*The Beast! The Beast is there!*

It was seen, hiding behind a wall; lying on its belly , stalking a young cowherd and his charges in a pasture. But, seemingly aware of its discovery, the Beast jumped the wall and reached the cover of a nearby copse.

The hunters converged, professional soldiers and a small peasant army, to surround the small wood. Some began to squeeze in between the branches...

The Beast suddenly broke cover, gaining momentum until it was felled by close range shot. It got up, received a second bullet and fell again, then it remorselessly rose once more and hobbled painfully into the woods. It attempted to break cover elsewhere meeting another staccato volley of well-placed shots, always falling but always getting up; until with the final rays of the setting sun it was seen going back into the undergrowth and disappearing...

A cordon was maintained during the night but no further contact was made. Believing the Beast to be dead or dying from its many bullet wounds, the search for its remains began in the morning. 200 well-armed men walked forward, line abreast and explored all the bushes, opening the branches, digging the piles of dead leaves, until it was learned that two women who'd come to watch the hunt, witnessed it limping away through nearby fields.

## August 31

Gadret had heard the myths of the region's celebrated monster through popular culture and was a little cynical about its authenticity. From the Bête's reign of terror had come tales of werewolves, Red Riding Hood and the demonization of wolves in general – and their extermination and extinction from continental France. It was a type of social hysteria. He had no doubt that the Beast had grown in stature, roamed ever-further and ever more terrible with each telling and retelling of   its story.

In the late nineteen-fifties and throughout the sixties and seventies accounts of alien abduction and UFO sightings had been common, then as suddenly as the Cold War ended so did these events. UFOs had become demystified phenomena – secret military aircraft, weather balloons, meteorological formations – and these strange accounts had been explained away as a strange manifestation of the psyche modelling reality from paranoia.

Nevertheless, ignoring the hysteria there were real events and occurrences that deserved investigation to uncover the occluded truth.

* * *

Gadret parked his car against the wall of the tumbled down church in Sainte Eulalie's square and walked through the alleyways until he reached a dilapidated farmhouse at the edge of the village.

He rang the doorbell after first checking the name 'Orlazabal' on the pale blue letterbox to ensure that he was at the right place. He noticed the chickens hanging inverted from the fence, still twitching as their lifeblood drained from their slit throats into an old enamel tub.

Eventually he heard footsteps approach from inside and a rough country voice challenged him, "Who are you, what do you want?"

Gadret pulled his warrant card from his leather jacket's inside pocket, "I am sergeant Gadret from the gendarmerie in Mende. I wondered if you'd spare me some time to tell me about the incident reported in the paper about the death of your hunting dog."

"That was nearly two months ago now. I told the reporters all there was to it. Anyhow since when have the police been interested in what happens to a hunting dog?" The voice was hostile; the man had still not come to the door.

"I am investigating the disappearance of the two foreign students near the gorge," Gadret explained.

A bolt slid and the door was pulled ajar, a rough looking overweight man dressed in soiled clothes appraised the gendarme with jaundiced eyes, "You'd better come in then."

Gadret hesitated, "Actually I'd hoped you'd show me where the incident took place, and talk me through it there."

* * *

Frederic Orlazabal smelled strongly of sweat, cow dung and garlic, the honest smells of a farmer, it wafted back, as he led Gadret over the pastures to the edge of the communal forest.

It was a bleak place; a high plateau some seventeen kilometres north of the gorge, even in the summer the wind blew cold and the ground was soggy underfoot.

From hostile, Orlazabal's attitude had changed to one of self-importance, he led the investigator along, carefully recounting the events of six weeks ago, much as Gadret had read in Sanchez' cuttings.

"I go hunting with the dog almost every Sunday. You can't beat a nice bit of game on your plate on a Sunday dinnertime. I go hunting while Madame Orlazabal goes to the church service. I used to go myself, but I don't care for this new priest we've got.

"Anyhow, on the Sunday in question I slipped the dog of his lead 'bout here," the farmer said waving his arms around about himself.

"What sort of dog was it?" asked Gadret, a little out of breath at trying to keep at the countryman's deceptively rapid pace.

"He was a hunting dog, not any sort of pedigree really, a cross between a setter and a griffon. He was a fair size though, about the same size as one of your police dogs," Orlazabal explained holding out his hand to show how tall the dog had stood, indicating that the dog was similar in stature to an Alsatian. "He just sort of went rooting around with his nose to the ground looking for fresh scent while I followed."

"What were you hunting?"

"Well, mostly I end up with a rabbit or two, some birds, or the odd hare, but I'm always hoping for a wild boar. I got one once, not far from here, the dog flushed him from the woods and I let him have it with both barrels. He kept the whole village in meat for nigh on a month!" The farmer stroked the stock of his gleaming double-barrelled shotgun as he recounted this story.

They reached a gate at the edge of the dark pine forest, which Orlazabal untied and opened.

He nodded up at the wooded slope; "He caught the scent of something just up there on the tree line. He went belting up the hill, baying his head off."

The farmer retied the gate and started up towards the trees, "I followed him as fast as I could, but there's no way I could keep up with him, I could just follow his howling."

* * *

The absolute silence and claustrophobic feeling within the trunks of the pines was unnerving. Footfalls fell onto a springing cushion of needles; the voice came out dull and dead, and once they had gone just a few metres into the trees the forest closed about them completely.

Orlazabal seemed certain of his path, he continued plunging into the forest, "I could hear the dog up ahead somewhere, then suddenly he started howling, then a yelp, then he was silent.

49

"I sort of knew something was wrong, I wondered if someone had maybe put out a gin trap. But without a sound to follow I just had to guess where he was..."

"How do you know where you are in a place like this?" Asked Gadret, now hopelessly disorientated.

The farmer pointed down at the moss-covered trunks of the trees, "The moss is always thickest and greenest on the south side of the tree."

Looking down Gadret could hardly see any difference in the growth, but he plunged on into the twilight world sticking closely to the heels of the farmer.

Orlazabal stopped suddenly at the edge of a small clearing, and brandished his shotgun. Gadret felt the hairs on the back of his neck rise, the green light was otherworldly, and the air temperature seemingly a few degrees lower. Ahead he could see that the gap in the canopy came about through the death of a tree, its great decaying trunk barring their path. "I found the dog there, by the tree, with his throat all slashed open," said Orlazabal, his face grim, his hands tightly gripping his shotgun.

While Orlazabal looked on, Gadret walked the scene methodically, his eyes scanning the ground around the area where the farmer had found the mutilated carcase of his dog.

He could find nothing unusual until he caught sight of something pale half buried in the mulch around the tree. He knelt down and picked up a small bone, extracted a small bag from his pocket and put it inside.

"What have you got there?" asked the farmer.

Gadret shrugged, "Probably nothing, just a bone." The Sergeant shivered involuntarily, "I think we've finished here."

"Thank God for that," growled Orlazabal "this place gives me the creeps!"

"The newspaper described your dog's injuries as deep slashes."

"Yes, that's right, he was ripped open across his chest and throat by what looked like a large claw with three talons," confirmed Orlazabal as he retied the gate.

"Do you think an animal could have done it?" asked Gadret.

The farmer scratched his stubbly chin, "Well, wild boar have got sharp tusks...But I don't think it was a pig. I'd have heard it squeal if it had been, and I can't think of anything else it could've been."

"What about a person?"

The farmer looked at the policeman in obvious astonishment. "Who the hell would be out in the woods in the middle of nowhere? What would they want to kill a dog for?"

Orlazabal looked at the policeman, his eyes wide and earnest, "You know I've never believed in those beast stories, I always said that there had to be some sort of logical explanation for them. But something in those woods killed my dog and it weren't some wolf or hyena, nor something that I've ever come across."

The farmer's eyes narrowed, "I think that maybe the old legends are right, there is some creature abroad in this god forsaken place, and it killed my dog!"

* * *

Maury pulled up outside the gîte.

Two girls were playing with cardboard boxes on a covered terrace, so absorbed in their game that they didn't see the Inspector until he greeted them and asked if their father was in.

The taller ran indoors and pulled a tired and plain looking woman by her hand to the door. "Someone to see you mummy." she said, running back to her game.

51

"Madame Abrages?" Asked Maury.

The woman looked suddenly worried as she nodded assent.

"I'm inspector Maury, a detective from Mende. I'm investigating the disappearance of the German students. I have to ask your husband some questions. It's nothing to worry about," He assured her, "It's just routine."

She looked a little less concerned and called into the house, "Daniel, there's a policeman here to see you."

Presently, Daniel Abrages emerged, a wiry man with a prominent beer belly, unfortunate buck teeth and shaved head. He looked nervous and seemingly unsure what to do with his hands as he thrust them into his trouser pockets.

"I wonder if you would answer a few questions for me Monsieur Abrages?"

Abrages nodded and stepped back into the house, Maury followed while Madame hissed at her girls to play quietly.

He showed Maury to a chair at the kitchen table.

The inspector read back the statement Abrages had made to the Gendarmes when he reported the students missing, and Abrages agreed that it was accurate.

"So the Golf was there both times you went to fish in the gorge?"

Abrages nodded.

"Did you catch anything?"

"Three salmon."

"Big ones?"

"Fair," said Abrages, pointing at a photograph hung from magnets on the fridge. It showed Abrages holding three large salmon aloft, while his wife and his two children beamed proud smiles.

"Where did you fish in the gorge?"

Abrages seemed to hesitate before answering, "In the ravine, near the waterfall."

"Did you see or hear anything in the gorge or ravine while you were there?"

Again the hesitation, and anxious movement of the hands before Abrages responded. "I saw the girl in the camp on the first day, she was reading a book outside her tent. That was on the way in. I saw no-one on the path to the gorge and no-one fishing the river. There was no-one to be seen at the camp on the way back to the car..."

"Did you hear anything?"

"No, the roar of the water is so loud in the gorge I take a music player and headphones with me."

Maury knew this statement to be true, but he felt that Abrages was holding something back. "Was there anything strange or out of place in the gorge or ravine?"

"...Well, actually I felt I was being watched as I fished, and followed as I returned to the car."

"But you didn't see anything or anyone?"

"No. I figured it was my imagination. It's a spooky place, the locals won't fish there."

Maury looked around the gîte, it was old fashioned and spartan. "Do you have a washing machine?" he asked.

"No." Abrages responded, looking puzzled.

"Then the clothes you wore fishing haven't been washed?"

"No, I don't think they have...I'll ask the wife.

"Julie," Abrages called, "You haven't washed my fishing gear yet have you?"

Madam Abrages poked her head in from the terrace, "No, I'm sorry I just haven't got around to it. It's in that shopping bag in the corner."

Abrages got up and retrieved the bag from the corner of the kitchen and thrust it at Maury. "I expect you'll be wanting to run tests on it?"

"Do you mind?" asked Maury.

"I got nothing to hide."

"Thank you, Monsieur Abrages, this should help rule you from our enquiries."

* * *

The bungalow was well kept, with a vivid array of annuals spilling from tubs placed at regular intervals around its detached grounds. Everything appeared to be in its proper place, Gadret noted as he pushed the intercom button under the name 'Heulot, E', next to the gate in the high wire fence that surrounded the place.

He was not surprised that the female voice that asked him his business also sounded neat - precise and measured.

"Gadret, sergeant Gadret, from the gendarmerie in Mende. I wondered if I might speak to Monsieur Heulot about his recent accident," he replied.

There was a brief pause, now the voice came back, a little ragged with anxiety, "There is no problem is there sergeant?"

"No Madame, I just have a few questions."

"Very well Sergeant. Monsieur Heulot will be out to unlock the gate for you in a few moments."

While he waited Gadret glanced over at the black Renault 16TXi parked against the fence on the far side of the compound. Except for damage to the nearside wing and door, the old car would have been in remarkable condition.

"Ah yes, it's a real pity!" remarked the sprightly old man who approached towards the gate from the dwelling in his slippers. He pointed towards the car, "I got it new in 1972, it never let me down. It still runs despite the accident, but the floor pan is buckled and my mechanic says it's a write-off!"

"Monsieur Heulot?"

"Call me Emile," confirmed the old man as he turned the key to unlock the gate, and glanced briefly at the Identity Card that Gadret held up for him to see. "How can I help you sergeant?"

Gadret nodded towards the damaged car, "Could you tell me about your accident?"

"Come inside," said Heulot motioning towards the highly polished front door.

* * *

Thank you Madame," said Gadret taking a cup of steaming tea from the silver tray. Heulot took his cup too, before his wife left them to converse in private.

They were sat on leather armchairs in the sitting room, a miniature poodle dozed on the rug between them, and the shining floor reflected the light pouring in from the French windows.

Heulot cleared his throat; "I was returning from Langogne, where I had attended a meeting of the Lions Club, I am the chairman you know. It is a small winding road between Langogne and Auroux and it passes through thick woodlands. It was quiet and I like to let the old girl have her head every now and again, so I suppose I must have been up to about eighty or ninety kilometres per hour on some stretches. Suddenly something appeared from the verge in front of me, a large animal, very strange looking and I swerved to avoid it. Unfortunately I lost control and the car fishtailed more and more wildly until one of the front wheels caught a kerb-stone and it span off the road."

55

Gadret noticed that the old man's hand trembled as he spoke.

"I was completely disoriented, my right foot was caught between the accelerator and brake pedal and the engine was screaming at full throttle. Somehow the impact had made the gearbox go into neutral, and my hand must have caught the switch to the headlamps, because only the sidelights and dashboard lights were on. It took me a few seconds to gather myself, but I managed to free my foot and to gather my thoughts. I realised then that the car had spun one hundred and eighty degrees and was facing down the road in the direction from which I had come. I was about to get out but then I remembered the animal that had made me swerve, so switched the headlamps onto full beam. There was the reflection of two sets of eyes a long way off in the verge but the lights didn't shine right onto any animal, but I could see one it although it was indistinct. It was large and light coloured, maybe grey, on all fours but high at the front, I thought for a moment that it was a wild boar, but it was too slender. I think the second one was further away in the trees. Within seconds it had slipped away and gone.

"I was too frightened to get out of the car, besides it was running alright so I drove it back onto the road and reversed until I found a place to turn it around then drove home. When I got here I telephoned the gendarmerie and my insurance agent to report the accident."

Heulot sipped his tea, his hand still trembling, "I was a captain in the army, based in Chad for nearly seven years, I have never seen such animals even in Africa, but the way it moved was more like a big cat. You know a fox or a dog will slip away happy for you to see its profile? But, like a cat this creature moved away by getting close to the ground, almost to melt into it, then slipping away backwards."

"How did the papers get your story?" Gadret asked.

"My insurance agent. He was drinking with a local reporter, said that la Bête had returned to the region!"

The sergeant fished a map from his pocket, "Do you think you could show me on this map where the incident happened?"

* * *

Maury gave the bag of fishing gear over to the desk sergeant with instructions for it to be analysed. "I also need a Search Warrant from the prosecuting judge."

"These are the details." he said handing over the address of the gîte in which the Abrages family was staying, "Tell him that Daniel Abrages was the last person to have seen the German student alive and that we can place him at both the camp-site and the location where the Italian student's body was found."

*T*wo days and three miles distant, a young man from Rimeize was found bleeding, scalped and his side torn open.

The same day, a child from Fontan was bitten to her cheek and to her arm;

Also found, in a field near the house of the de Morangiès family, the shredded remains of a 21-year-old girl whose parents had forced to go and milk the cows.

September 1

Maury thought of his grown-up children. He knew they, like Fabienne Sonnester, had faced severe financial pressures as studied and clawed their way up the social scale.

His eldest daughter had studied at university. Away from home she'd engaged in a risky lifestyle – the naïve and pretty country-girl, easily-led and gullible had a string of less than desirable boyfriends. Then she'd managed to get herself pregnant by a young entrepreneur she'd met at a party.

She though, had been fortunate, the young entrepreneur had proved to be a gentleman who of his own accord had stood by her in her decision to forgo her studies and keep the child. He'd maintained her financially, and their relationship had turned into friendship, respect and ultimately to a loving and secure marriage.

She had been lucky, maybe Fabienne Sonnester would have been lucky, if she'd not met a monster in the woods.

* * *

"So you had a busy weekend sergeant?" asked Maury, hanging his wet overcoat on the peg behind the door.

Gadret looked up from the laptop display at his superior, "Not really. Did you?"

The Inspector held out his arm and let a yellow forensics report glide onto the desk between them, "Obviously less busy than yours sergeant!"

Gadret looked at the report and held his breath.

"If you thought that Sanchez was onto something you should have said so. There are two of us on this investigation Gadret!" Maury leaned over the desk, his eyes boring into Gadret's his disappointment and simmering anger quite obvious.

"But I thought you made it clear that you thought his theory wasn't

59

worth serious consideration," reminded Gadret.

"True, but you obviously thought it was, and you should have let me know that."

"Yes Sir."

Maury's gaze fell to the yellow paper in Gadret's hand and he relaxed visibly, "The little bone you found happens to be human, a finger bone in fact. So maybe your professor's theory is not quite so eccentric after all. Not only is it human but, as you see, we have a DNA match with our missing fisherman from Pradelles."

* * *

Gadret led the forensics teams across the fields from Sainte Eulalie in the tracks of Orlazabal's tractor, Maury riding in the link box with the team's heavier equipment as it swung wildly over the rough ground. The Inspector hung on grimly, regretting his decision to accept the farmer's lift, as the large wheels dug into the saturated ground and spewed a stream of sour mud over his legs from the deep treads.

At last the roaring engine quietened and the hydraulic arms lowered the link-box to the ground. Orlazabal shouted from the cab, "You need to open the gate!"

Grateful to be able to return to terra firma, Maury squelched to earth and circled around the great agricultural monster and pulled open the steel gate to let it pass.

Belching black fumes from its upright exhaust, Orlazabal steered the snarling machine through the narrow gap with nonchalant ease. Maury waved him on when the farmer looked back; from here he now preferred to walk to the looming pine forest.

The tractor laboured up the steep rise, its wheels scrabbling for traction, then stopped at the treeline. Orlazabal jumped from the cab and lit a cigarette as he watched Maury breathlessly propel his overweight body up the slope.

At the dense treeline the inspector looked around himself, the place was as forsaken and lonely as Gadret had said, especially with the wind making the pines brush together with an inevitable cracking of branches.

The search team following each other single file across the fields were dwarfed by the sheer scale of the landscape, even the giant tractor looked insignificant against the great shoulder of the massif.

Orlazabal offered a Camel, which Maury declined, "What are you hoping to find inspector?"

"Clues," He stated simply.

It took some time to organise the search team, they had first to follow the farmer into the forest and then, when near the site of the fallen tree, to spread out in line abreast through the trunks to walk the scene.

This first sweep revealed nothing within fifty metres of the tree, so great lamps were erected by technicians so that a detailed examination of the great reclining trunk and its tangle of branches could continue in the half light and darkness. Then specialists clad in overalls set to work, while a huddle of other policemen cordoned the area with tape to keep the encroaching gloom of the forest at bay.

Gadret approached carrying two polystyrene cups, "Coffee Sir?" he enquired.

With the chill of evening in the air Maury was glad of the hot beverage.

He turned his collar up, and both men turned to watch the ghost-like forms of the men in white methodically mapping and examining the area within the cordon. Then they saw one of the team raise a hand to be rapidly joined by several of his companions.

Maury's radio crackled to life, "Sir, we've found something in the mulch under the branches...Bones, human bones, ulna, humerus...a human forearm."

**W**hat was now certain, was that the Beast was not a wolf.

Too many people had seen it and given the same description: it was a fantastic animal, as large as a calf or a donkey; it had reddish hair, a large head similar to a pig, the mouth always gaping, short and perched ears, deep chested with a tapering rear end. Some said that its hind legs wore hooves of a horse.

September 2

She knew in herself that her running had become an addiction, it came before all else in her life – except the wolves.

Laura had often been asked what her fascination was towards these fierce untameable beasts. Her answers it seemed, even to herself, would change because there was no easy answer. But she knew that secretly she harboured an affinity with the creatures. They were hard, spare endurance athletes who seemed assured of their place in the world.

She had been a naturalist since a childhood spent in French Guyana. Moving from the Americas to study in Europe had at first seemed a taming experience, but her interest in French native wildlife had been piqued after a visit to the Pyrenees with its bears, wolves and vultures living cheek by jowl with tolerant humans. When the opportunity to work the re-establishment of wolves into their erstwhile stronghold of Gevaudan had arisen, she jumped at the chance.

And now she was addicted – to running and to wolves.

* * *

Once more the large-scale map was spread across Maury's desk, the inspector jabbed his finger at a light blue shape.

"This is the lake where Alain Descartes disappeared," Maury dragged his finger a long way over the map, "And this is where we found the remains of his forearm."

He looked into the faces of his companions.

Gadret was focussed on details of the map, his eyes tracing contours and footpaths. Beside the Sergeant stood a triumphant looking Sanchez and opposite him, a drawn-looking Platigny who was shaking her dark blonde head in disbelief, "There is no way that one of our escaped grey wolves did this!" the wolf expert protested.

"You will have the opportunity to prove that." Said Maury. "I'd like you to join a team to locate your missing wolves."

Laura Platigny looked stunned, "I'm not equipped for that sort of thing!" she protested.

"Nonsense," said Maury dismissively, "You are the best fell-runner in France, and you have been on numerous expeditions to study wolves. Have you not?"

Platigny nodded, "What sort of team?" she asked with resignation.

"Legionnaires...a training exercise for specialist trackers, you have a squad of fourteen at your disposal and a helicopter."

"For how long?" asked Platigny.

"Four days."

"I don't know if that will be enough time." Protested Platigny.

"Oh, I think it will be." Said Maury sliding a buff envelope across the table, "Eight of your trackers are Siberians."

Maury now turned to Gadret and Sanchez. "Professor, I'd like you to assist Sergeant Gadret and myself while we investigate the incidents you have so exhaustively collated.

"Gadret will concentrate on sightings and livestock attacks while I investigate any missing persons that you think could be attributed to the Beast. We shall start with the most recent first."

* * *

Maury held Gadret back until Sanchez and Platigny had left the office.

He passed a folder over to the sergeant. "It's a search warrant for the gîte where Daniel Abrages, the fisherman is staying. He gave us the clothes he was wearing for forensic examination, which revealed nothing. I don't know what part he's played in all this but he's definitely not coming clean about something. So, we'll make a start with him before we get on with Sanchez' list."

* * *

The search of the gîte revealed nothing.

The two Crime Scene investigators had soon gone through the house and its contents. However, Abrages had visibly shrivelled when they removed his laptop for examination. He followed Maury outside to his car, obviously nervous.

"Is something worrying you Daniel?" Maury asked.

Abrages looked back at the house nervously, "I have private things on that laptop." he said,

"What sort of things?"

Abrages hung his head, "Porn." he said in a whisper.

"What sort of pornography?" Maury asked.

"Not anything with kids or animals...just kinky stuff..." Abrages stammered.

"Then you've nothing to worry about Daniel."

"Does my wife need to know?"

"That's up to you."

"You won't tell her?"

"It's your business Daniel, if it's nothing illegal you've nothing to worry about."

Abrages looked reassured, "Alright then."

*I*t seemed the Beast could be everywhere at once; in the same day it could appear in places separated by 6 to 7 miles.

*It liked to stand up on its hind legs, cross rivers in two or three jumps and walk on the water without getting wet.*

*A reliable witness attested that he had heard the Beast laugh and speak.*

*Moreover, it rarely devoured the corpse of its victims, contenting itself with tearing it apart, sucking its blood, scalping its head and devouring the heart, the liver and the intestines.*


*It was a time of glut for the Beast. It showed itself daily and deprived its appetite of nothing. The list of its slaughter is frightening: in the village of La Clause, it devoured, a young girl, Gabrielle Peissier, and arranged her body so cleanly that one, at first thought the girl was only asleep.*

*On April 18th, it killed a 12 year-old cowherd, bleeding him dry as a butcher would have done, eating his cheeks, his eyes, his thighs and dislocating his knees. In Ventuejols, it slashed the throat of a 40 year-old woman then her two little girls before bleeding them dry and pulling out their hearts.*

*There are few villages in the Gévaudan whose parish registers do not bear, in this spring of 1765, many sinister entries of this kind: "Death certificate of the body of…eaten partially by the ferocious Beast…"*

*The Beast seemed indestructible: widely seen, easily tracked, shot, hounded, poisoned and still returning to civilization for its prey. It flaunted its presence seeming to revel in the terror it inspired. Several times it was seen at a distance, by its would be ambushers, to gambol gaily as if it wanted to taunt its future victims.*

September 3

Laura had often pondered the Bête du Gevaudan enigma. When in contact with the public at the Marvejols Wolf Park she had often been asked if the mysterious beast could have been a rogue wolf.

While it was true that wolves had roamed the region and isolated attacks had been relatively common in France until as recently as 1918, attacks by a single lone wolf upon a number of human victims was rare.

The celebrated Sarlat Wolf which had attacked and wounded seventeen adult men in June 1766 was now broadly accepted to have been a dog/wolf hybrid. Like the Bête du Gevaudan, it was reported to have attacked standing on its hind legs to bite at face or neck.

A more likely candidate, from the descriptions of witnesses in the period of the attacks in Lozère, was a hyena. Although not native to Europe, at that time the gentry often visited French colonies in Africa and returned with exotic specimens, perhaps someone had returned with a Spotted Hyena.

The Spotted Hyena is a recognised man-eater, and man-eating hyena are typically very large: a pair responsible for killing at least twenty-seven people in Malawi in 1962 weighed in at seventy-two and seventy-seven kilograms. The behaviour of the Bête also emulated that of man-eating hyena in that they are known to attack people in their dwellings in broad daylight. Like the Bête these hyena predate mainly women, children and sick, old or infirm men.

In 2004 a World Wildlife Fund report indicated that a solitary hyena killed thirty-five people in a very localised area on the border of Mozambique and Tanzania.

* * *

The helicopter swept over treetops swaying in the down-wash from the rotors. Legionnaires sat with their legs dangling from the open doors, unconcerned by the steep banking of the aircraft as it hugged the contours of the landscape.

Laura sat next to the officer, well away from the yawning gaps of open doors on either side of the fuselage, shivering in the blast of the wind that tugged at her camouflaged fatigues, and tried not to look at the ground rushing by just a few metres under the whirling blades.

Soon the helicopter touched down at the edge of boggy ground and the legionnaires dropped from its skids and squatted low under the mechanical gale that flattened the long grass around them.

Laura followed the officer as he too alighted from the craft. Then the olive helicopter was climbing away in a long climbing turn under the grey clouds, spewing rank smoke from its hard-working engines.

Meanwhile, the soldiers went about a well-rehearsed and silent routine, checking weapons and equipment before four detached themselves from their companions to quarter the landing area.

The officer turned to Laura jabbing a finger at a point on his plastic-covered map, "We are here. This is the area where wolves were supposedly seen a couple of days ago."

With a subtle gesture a nearby soldier caught the officer's attention and pointed towards one of the four soldiers who were quartering the area.

"Follow me mademoiselle," the officer directed.

Platigny was led to a soldier kneeling to examine the ground. The soldier pointed at indistinct marks in the mud, the tricolour of France resplendent on his outstretched arm.

"Wolf tracks?" asked the officer.

Platigny looked closely at the faint indentations in the earth, and nodded.

Two other soldiers, one a corporal, arrived and squatted down to examine the tracks closely conferring with one another in a softly spoken language that Laura supposed was Russian.

The corporal made his report to the officer in halting French, "Wolf tracks, yes. Perhaps forty-eight hours old, three or four animals."

\* \* \*

Maury looked around at the bright naïve drawings that decorated the corridor as he waited for Madame Tournant to be summoned; he marvelled at the quietness of the school during lesson time, he had expected the place to be noisy.

The tip tap of heels on the shiny wooden floor alerted him to the schoolteacher's presence. He looked around and watched the petite woman approach, he smiled and saw the tension in her tight face and shoulders dissipate.

After brief introductions in the corridor Madame Tournant led him into a well-appointed office, ushered the policeman into a seat, closed the door and sat opposite, crossing her exquisitely formed legs. "How can I help you Inspector?" Her lips were bright red and curled at the edges as if on the brink of a smile though her blue eyes were intense and serious.

Maury passed the teacher a small photograph from his wallet, "Do you recognise this girl?"

Madame Tournant's response was immediate. "Yes," she replied, "this is Annalise Rrukaj." Her pretty brow furrowed. "Have you any news of her?"

Maury took back the photograph and shook his head. "No. I was hoping that you might be able to help me, I am re-examining her disappearance in the course of some other investigations."

Madame Tournant looked at him levelly, flicking a blonde strand from her cheek. "I think I told the investigating officers all I could back at the time."

"And nothing's changed since?"

"No...there were some silly rumours circulating amongst some of the girls a couple of months ago, but nothing of any consequence."

"What were these rumours?"

The teacher shrugged, "Girls that age are full of mischief, some were saying that Annalise had been kidnapped by her uncle and others that she had been murdered."

"What do you think?"

The schoolteacher looked into space and gathered her thoughts, her hands clenching on the hem of her pencil skirt, "She was last seen walking towards her friend's house, anyone could have picked her up and taken her."

"Is Annalise's friend here at the school?"

Madame Tournant nodded.

"Was she involved in any of this gossip?"

"No...not directly, but some of her friends were."

"Could I speak to her?" Maury pulled on his glasses and consulted his notebook, "It's Marie-Claude Virogny isn't it?"

"Not without her parent's permission."

* * *

Gadret looked down at the list stapled to the burgundy folder that Sanchez had made him, and scratched through the name Dupond. He looked up at the dilapidated blue house front to see Dupond's wife peeking from behind the soiled lace curtains.

As he started the car's engine he hoped his next visit would not be as fruitless as this morning's four previous. In each case it was obvious that the sightings were fanciful and so fleeting as to be useless. He checked the next name and address on his list before engaging low gear and moving off.

* * *

Marie-Claire held Madame Tournant's hand as she was ushered into the office. She towered over the teacher, tall and thin, but otherwise undeveloped for her age, without a distinct female shape. Her striking red hair was in plaits that swung across her back as she sat into the chair opposite, and her mouth was full of stainless steel braces.

"Hello Marie-Claire, my name is inspector Maury. Your mum and dad have said it's all right for me to ask you about your friend Annalise. Would that be okay with you?"

The girl nodded demurely.

"How long have you and Annalise been friends?"

"Since she came to this school, about two years ago."

"Are you best friends?"

Marie-Claire nodded, "Yes, I think so."

"Do you know what happened to her?"

Marie-Claire looked down at her hands and remained silent.

Maury continued, "Madame Tournant tells me that there were rumours that Annalise may have been kidnapped. There were other stories too, have you heard any of them?"

The girl nodded, but still looked down at her hands. Suddenly she sobbed and large tears fell onto her tightly clasped fingers.

"It's alright Marie-Claire," comforted Madame Tournant softly as she put an arm around the girl's shoulder.

"I've promised to say nothing," wailed the girl.

Madame Tournant shot Maury a shocked glance.

"You made a promise?" asked the Inspector, "Was it to Annalise?"

The girl's nod was almost imperceptible.

"So Annalise rang you?" Maury asked Marie-Claire, "When?"

Madame Tournant assured the girl, "It's alright Marie-Claire, you won't get into trouble for telling the Inspector the truth."

Hesitantly Marie-Claire confirmed the revelation, "She rang me about three weeks after she disappeared."

"What did she say?"

"She told me she was alright, that her family had to move away from France in a hurry and that her uncle had picked her up on her way to my place."

"Did she tell you where she was?"

"She said that they were on their way to England."

"What did you say to her?"

"I told her that everyone thought something horrible had happened to her. She started crying and saying that she didn't want to leave with her family, that she felt as if she'd been taken against her will."

* * *

The slope was barren of all but scrubby tussocks of bleached grass poking through the dark peaty earth.

Laura struggled to maintain the pace of the soldiers, who despite being loaded with equipment moved with fluid ease over the rough ground. They were well spread out and Platigny only caught rare glimpses of camouflaged men patrolling on the periphery and the soldier bringing up the rear-guard. Their relentless pace and stamina impressed the naturalist, they reminded her of wolves, and she could now see why man was the only predator those magnificent animals feared.

* * *

The end of the farm lane was hard to find, the sign that marked it overgrown with brambles. The car grounded on stones several times but Gadret eventually reached the range of farm buildings. He parked in a farmyard swimming in slurry, his arrival announced by the barking of a couple of mangy dogs.

A stocky woman in a shapeless mud-spattered dress, wearing curious rubber clogs appeared from a dark doorway. Her lip curled in disgust as she recognised the police car and watched Gadret alight, his shiny boots squelching in the liquid dung. "Madame Charriere?" Gadret called.

"What do you want?" The woman's tone was hostile, challenging.

"I'm sergeant Gadret from the gendarmerie in Mende, I wondered if I could ask you a few questions."

"What about?"

"The wolves your husband was said to have shot."

"What?" The woman's tone was incredulous, disbelieving, and her jaw slackened, "Then you'll be wanting to speak to Monsieur Charriere. I'll get him for you."

She reached into a pocket and brought a top-of-the-line mobile phone to her ear, "Emile, you'd better get down to the yard there's a policeman here to see you."

Monsieur Charriere was a fat, jolly man who seemed delighted to see Gadret. Ordering his wife to continue seeing to the livestock, the farmer led the sergeant to the grey-tiled farmhouse. He took his wellingtons off at the door and Gadret did likewise before being ushered into a bright, clean and thoroughly modern kitchen.

They sat at the table, Charriere pouring two small glasses of red wine.

"You are reported to have seen wolves on your land."

Charriere laughed, "Several times!"

"Eight wolves escaped from the wolf park in Marvejols last year, we are trying to account for them all. How many did you see?"

The farmer scratched his stubbly double chin, "Six, they were attacking my flock."

73

"You shot two?"

"Yes."

"What happened to the others?"

"They ran off."

"You said you'd seen them several times."

Charriere nodded, "Yes, usually far-off on the tree-line."

"Was that before or after you'd shot at them?"

"Both, I saw the six a couple of times before then, and I've seen the four since."

"How many times were your livestock attacked?"

"Just the once."

"What did you do with the bodies of the wolves you shot?"

"I hung them up on a fence."

"Why?"

"To scare the others off the farm, we do it with crows and buzzards too."

"Are they still there?"

"I think so, I'll take you up there if you want to see them."

* * *

The desiccated and flyblown remains of the two wolves still hung upon the gruesomely decorated barbed-wire fence. Leathery pelts still stuck grimly to the bleaching bones, on the eyeless heads the lips had retreated to reveal the sharp white canines.

"Well, there they are," stated Charriere proudly, "Might appear a ghastly practice but it kept the others away."

Gadret said nothing; he put on surgical gloves and reached into his pocket for a couple of thick black bin liners.

* * *

Lieutenant Danczjac led Laura into a tangle of windblown trees and pointed into a hollow hidden away under the branches. There lay the remains of an animal with the pale bones of a ribcage easy to identify in the gloom.

"Deer?" queried Platigny.

The officer nodded, "A young male, a good meal for the wolves we are tracking. The trackers say it was killed and eaten yesterday."

* * *

In the dull light that washed into his office from the window Maury pored over Annalise Rrukaj's file, his eyes scanning the data.

There was little information about the girl's family, and Mende's community of illegal immigrants had refused to assist in a police investigation that began when Marie Claire Virogny's family had signalled the girl's disappearance. Annalise had failed to turn up to her friend's for a prearranged sleepover.

After the police publicised the girl's disappearance a witness came forward who said he thought he saw a girl being bundled into a car on the road between Mende and the Virogny family home.

Two other witnesses claimed to have seen a large wolf-like creature in the area at the same time; it was their claim that had triggered the press into sensationalising the case into an attack by the returning 'Bête du Gevaudan'.

The investigation stalled when no-one other than the Virogny family reported Annalise's disappearance, apparently her own family - thought to be Albanian - had not come forward.

Maury reached for the phone, "Could you put me through to Customs please operator?"

An accommodating customs officer seemed pleased to be able to help, "Yes, we were investigating several immigrants who were living and working illegally in Mende last year," confirmed the Customs officer.

"Any Albanian?" Maury asked.

"Yes, several."

"Does the name Rrukaj ring a bell?"

"Can you spell that?"

"R-R-U-K-A-J."

Maury could hear keys tapping in the background, before the man spoke again, "There's a Ruka."

"Ruka?"

"Henri Ruka."

"Have you got an address?"

More tapping, "45bis Rue Hotchkiss."

Maury ran his finger under the last known address of the missing schoolgirl Annalise Rrukaj - 45 Rue Hotchkiss. "I will need to see the file to aid a missing persons investigation."

"No problem Inspector, the file is closed, I'll send you a copy if you like."

"The file is closed you say?"

"Yes, the investigating officers closed the file when Ruka couldn't be traced, they suspect he moved on to Germany or England."

"Thank you, you've been most helpful, please get the file to me as soon as you can."

When the file arrived Maury printed it out and read it page by page using a yellow highlighter to pick out key points. The information included field reports from investigating officers that seemed to confirm that the Ruka/Rrukaj family were one and the same. The family were said to be either Albanian or Macedonian, the father Enrik was working for a gang who subcontracted forestry work, the mother was seldom seen except when shopping. The description of the elder daughter fitted Annalise exactly.

Amongst the notes were brief descriptions of the family's visitors and the cars they drove. One entry immediately caught Maury's eye - just days prior to the girl's disappearance the family were visited by a couple driving a German registered Volkswagen Golf. A large buff envelope contained photographs, under the magnifying glass Maury could just make out the registration number of the silver GTI the DO prefix showed it was Dortmund registered.

It was not Fabienne Sonnester's car, yet Maury wondered if Annalise's and the German student's disappearances were related in any other way. Perhaps Fabienne's shady past had caught up with her, the connection must be in Dortmund.

* * *

The smell from the bags was revolting; here in the enclosed laboratory the nostrils were assaulted by the undiluted stench of putrefying flesh. A forensics technician poked around in the tangle of pelt and bones while Gadret watched.

The man pulled at an eyeless head, found the rumpled remains of an ear and examined it closely; he raised his eyes to Gadret's and nodded. "F48M022F," He said.

Gadret noted the number, already knowing that the tattoo identified the dead wolf as one that escaped from Marvejols.

The technician found the identifying tattoo on the second pelt, "F48M104F."

Again the number indicated that the second wolf also came from Marvejols, Gadret noted this number too.

* * *

77

The glow of the small stove and the mug of sweet tea she clutched brought welcome warmth to Laura Platigny's tired and aching body. She watched as soldiers moved effortlessly around her in another well-drilled routine, erecting low bivouacs in the shelter of a fold in the hill.

Danczjac detached himself from the men and squatted on his haunches next to the naturalist. "Good news, we have found fresher tracks ahead. The wolves are just a day ahead of us."

"I thought I was fit before today," admitted Laura, "But I don't think I can keep up today's pace for another day."

"You are a fell runner aren't you? Sergeant Gadret said you were a champion."

"This is different."

The lieutenant smiled, "It's okay Mademoiselle Platigny, you won't have to keep up. There are four specialist trackers ahead of us. They will track the wolves and call us when the time comes to intercept them. We will be picked up by helicopter to join them."

"You mean that there are still men out there tracking the wolves?" Asked Platigny incredulously.

The officer laughed, "They are in their element Mademoiselle Platigny."

* * *

The forensics officer came into the office with Abrages laptop.

"Anything?" asked Maury.

"Nothing illegal, just this..." said the officer switching the device on.

It was hardcore porn produced by Eurorevenue in Germany, a masked blonde girl performing sexual acts with a number of men. Despite the mask the girl was unmistakeably Fabienne Sonnester.

*O*ne particular incident moved the whole of France.

*A twelve-year-old shepherd boy from Chanaleilles, named Jacques Portefaix, was looking after cattle in the mountains. With him were four friends and two little girls. Fearful of being attacked by the Beast the children had armed themselves with iron-pointed sticks.*

*Suddenly, one of the little girls shouted in alarm, the Beast had appeared from a bush next to her. Jacques Portefaix gathered the little band, with the stronger boys protecting the rest. The monster circled them, its mouth frothing.*

*Huddled together, the courageous children crossed themselves piously and prepared to defend themselves with their sticks. Unperturbed the Beast dashed forward, grabbing 8-year-old Joseph Panafieux by the throat and attempted to drag him away. Jacques tried valiantly to protect his friend, stabbing at the Beast repeatedly in an attempt to force it to drop its prey. In the struggle Joseph's cheek was torn off and while he scrabbled back to his friends the Beast nonchalantly dined upon it.*

*The Beast appeared to be animated at the taste, rearing up it began re-attacking the horrified group, knocking over one of the little girls. Snapping wildly with terrible fangs it latched onto one of the boys, Jean Veyrier, by his lips, pulled him to the ground, altered its purchase to his arm and dragged him away.*

*One boy saw this as their opportunity to escape, they could flee while the monster was busy pulling the unfortunate Jean apart. But Jacques declared that they would save their friend's life or die trying. So, the children followed Jacques, even Joseph blinded by his blood and missing one cheek, and they rushed upon the Beast.*

*Catching up with it, they frantically laid into the Beast's head, trying to burst its eyes or to cut its tongue. It backed itself into ditch where it got bogged in foul-smelling mud and released the Veyrier boy. Jacques fearlessly placed himself between the Beast and its dropped prey, hitting the Beast's bloody snout so that finally it stepped back, shook itself and loped away.*

*All over France, the newspapers headlines and lurid images described this epic fight; Jacques Portefaix became an immediate celebrity - but so also did the Beast.*

September 4

Men and wolves have much in common, their lives revolve around the family unit.

Laura could imagine men and wolves colonising the steppe together as the ice-cap retreated from northern lands after the Ice Age. Both were clever hunters, working co-operatively on the hunt, both persistent and enduring, both tenacious and ultimately succeeding against heavier and fiercer prey through intelligence and attrition. Little wonder then that these two species had been drawn together in those vast cold wastelands.

Perhaps wolves had been drawn to man's fireside to share warmth and company after the day's hunt. And some it seems must have remained among the other's pack to become domesticated – the dog – protector, companion and friend. Laura pondered this and man's strange attitude – his hostility toward the untamed wolf and his love of the dog.

What was also fascinating, to Laura, was the folklore and myth that the wolf shared with man. Throughout history, it seems that the two species have shared a symbiotic relationship. Remus and Romulus, the infant founders of Rome were foundlings succoured by a she-wolf, Kipling's boy hero Mowgli was also raised by wolves, with Lord Baden-Powell modelling his Cub-Scout movement upon Akela's wolf-pack. The wolf was a common totem of hunter-gatherer tribes in the Americas and Eurasia where it is still the National symbol of the Chechen peoples. Saint Francis of Assisi was an unlikely champion of the wolf, the Norse god Odin was said to take the form of a wolf.

But where people established farming and agriculture the wolf has become a pariah, a symbol of evil – a glutton that kills, but seldom to eat. The wolf becomes the enemy of the pastoral flock – an incarnation of the Devil himself.

* * *

Laura was shaken awake, "It is time to get up Mademoiselle." said lieutenant Danczjac.

Laura's eyes soon adjusted to the gloom, she got her bearings and wriggled free of the sleeping bag. Her whole body felt sore and stiff as she crawled out of the low bivouac into the crisp grey of the false dawn.

A legionnaire thrust a cup of strong coffee at her, while two others worked quickly to strike camp.

The lieutenant knelt on his haunches and shone the beam of his torch onto a map, he pointed at smudges that depicted mountains and forests, "We are here, the trackers are about 25 kilometres away here... and they are going to chase the wolves into this valley here. It narrows at the col, that is where we shall be dropped by helicopter in order to ambush them." The torch clicked off, "The helicopter will be here in about fifteen minutes."

Platigny cradled the hot cup in her hands and shivered as cold air picked at her exposed flesh. Around her the legionnaires had struck camp and now sat on their rucksacks, looking at her with furtive glances, talking in low whispers as they checked the actions of their high velocity rifles and adjusted the sights. Self-consciously Laura realised that her tight t-shirt poorly disguised her cold-hardened nipples.

* * *

The helmeted policemen in green overalls waited for the detective in the black leather coat to give them the nod.

Ludwig checked his notebook. Then, happy that they stood outside the right apartment he gave the signal. The sledgehammer broke the lock and the armed policemen rushed into the dark interior shouting "Polizei!"

Ludwig followed and found the light switch.

In the sudden glare the occupants of the tiny flat were revealed sleeping upon every piece of furniture and upon the floor. Men, women and children looked up in fear at the officers who shone torches into their faces.

Ludwig crossed over to one of the children, a dark-haired girl. "What is your name?" the detective asked gently.

The girl looked at a nearby woman, obviously her mother, who nodded. "Annalise Rrukaj,." the girl whispered.

* * *

The arrival of the helicopter surprised Laura who had expected it to roar over the treetops, instead the drab machine had materialised from below the horizon with a whisper.

Holding their forage caps against the prop wash the legionnaires ran forward and started throwing equipment to a waiting load-master within the dark fuselage door. The lieutenant ushered Laura forward and she was propelled without ceremony into the body of the aircraft.

The naturalist found herself a spot to sit with her back against the forward bulkhead, a spot that she felt would be more sheltered from the gale of prop wash and well clear of the yawning fuselage doors.

The motors rose in pitch and the helicopter began lifting as soon as the last legionnaire was aboard. Laura was glad she was well inboard when the aircraft pitched and banked to follow the contours of the ground and she caught occasional glimpses of treetops rushing by, just centimetres from the rotor tips.

She was glad to have her feet back on solid ground; the movement of the helicopter had made her feel very unwell. Now she and the legionnaires were clambering over rising ground to the narrow col in which they were to lay in ambush for the wolves.

At the col Laura called Danczjac over, opened her rucksack and handed the officer the specially made tranquilliser darts. The lieutenant called his sharpshooters over one by one and personally loaded a dart carefully into the breach of their rifles. Then he called two other legionnaires over and spoke to them in Russian.

He turned back to Platigny as these two soldiers made their way back down the slope. "If the snipers miss, those two will destroy the animals with automatic weapons."

At Laura's look of horror Danczjac smiled and lightly put his hand on the naturalist's forearm, "Don't worry...they won't miss."

* * *

Maury's wife answered the telephone ringing in the hall while he sat at the kitchen table spreading apricot jam onto his croissants.

"It's for you," she said as she looked around the door.

Maury rose slowly to his feet, careful to see that all the crumbs were folded into his napkin before he placed it on the table.

"Allo? Inspector Maury speaking"

A heavily accented voice spoke in English, "This is captain Ludwig of the Dortmund police."

"Ah?..Dortmund? Yes, of course. How did it go Captain?"

"I am glad to say that we found the Rrukaj girl safe and well," the captain reported.

"That's great!"

"She was with the uncle's family."

"It's definitely Annalise?"

"Yes, there is no doubt that it is Annalise."

"That is very good news captain Ludwig."

"Yes, but there is a problem..."

"What is that?" Maury asked.

"It is the father Enrik who disappeared."

"Say again?"

"The family say they left France because the father never returned from work, they say that he went to work in the morning and did not return. They seem frightened of something, but they will not speak. I am afraid I cannot help you more."

"What of the other matter?"

"The film-makers Eurorevenue?"

"Yes."

"My colleague visited the company. Fabienne Sonnester worked for them twice under a pseudonym, that is normal they say, and she was paid for her services. She did not provide them with a contact number or address."

"Was there anyone there she knew?"

"It seems not."

"Can you be sure?"

"Not absolutely, but what was unusual and what made the company remember her is that she brought a contract for them to sign, usually it is the other way around."

"What sort of contract?"

"Preserving and reinforcing her right to anonymity, apparently she even arrived, worked and left in disguise and the studio could not even reveal her pseudonym."

"She covered her tracks. Can you be sure it was her?"

"The bank account details agree. She was paid by bank transfer. I think we can be pretty sure."

"Thank you captain, thanks once again for your help."

Maury hung up and returned to his breakfast.

* * *

Maury opened the envelope containing Gadret's reports.

So far the sergeant had visited and interviewed seven witnesses who claimed to have seen wolves or wolf-like creatures. His investigations had led to the recovery of the remains of two dead Marvejols wolves.

What was apparent was that the most consistent and reliable reports came from witnesses living in isolation some way from hamlets and villages. Five reports came from farmers who had lost livestock, of these only two claimed to have properly seen the creatures responsible and both named wolves. These two attacks were witnessed in broad daylight and both were upon lambs in lambing season. The other attacks were nocturnal, upon either cattle or sheep and the creatures responsible were either described as wolves, large cats or large wolf-like creatures.

Then he rose, put on his coat and summoned an officer to assist in his arrest of Daniel Abrages.

* * *

Even in this wild region, the hamlet of Espradels was a remote place, its houses spread individually over sombre north-facing slopes. None of the houses were marked, so Gadret pulled his car on to the driveway of a dilapidated farmhouse.

He wound down the window and called to a figure stooping among maize stalks, "Hello, I wonder if you could direct me to the Estoup farm?"

The figure rose stiffly and the man removed his beret to reveal a startlingly white bald head against his darkly tanned face. "You've found it," the man stated, "How can I help?"

Estoup was an amiable type; he seemed only too pleased to have a visitor. Gadret was ushered into the kitchen and sat down with a glass of red wine at the long pine table while the farmer recounted his assortment of strange events in the area. "Every winter I have livestock taken, usually a bullock or a sheep. Its remains will be found on the tree line, head, hooves and entrails if it's a bullock, or just entrails if it's a sheep. I do believe I saw the beast that done it; a couple of years back, by my eyes aren't what they used to be. It was hard to see it, because it stayed low in the trees. It was large and had grey fur on top and brown lower down. I never got a good view, mostly because seeing it started me shaking with fear."

"Don't you keep your livestock in the barns, during winter?" asked Gadret.

"Most of the time. But they have to be mucked out some time, usually on a brighter day, so the animals are let out into the paddock. Besides its good for them, and the cold kills some of the germs," explained Estoup.

"And they get taken from the paddock in daytime?"

"Well, no! It's more like dusk or in poor light that they get taken."

"Don't your dogs bark or the animals make any sort of noise?" asked Gadret looking at the two mongrels curled at Estoup's feet.

Estoup shook his head, "Not that I've noticed."

"Has anyone tried to track it?"

The farmer shook his head, "Not that I know of."

It transpired that Estoup's neighbours in the hamlet had also had livestock taken in the same manner during the winter months. When asked if any of them had claimed to see the animal responsible Estoup shook his head, "They don't believe in painting the devil on the wall around here."

Gadret asked what the saying meant. Estoup chuckled, "They think that if they admit that it could be the Beast, then it will turn out to be the Beast - a self-fulfilling prophecy!"

"Over how many years have these attacks on the livestock taken place?"

Estoup scratched at the pale pate under his beret, "About fifteen years by my reckoning."

"Fifteen years? Are you certain?" queried Gadret. If true then the escaped Marvejols wolves could not be to blame.

"Yes, I'm pretty sure, about fifteen or sixteen years."

Something niggled at Gadret; he could not understand why none of the farmers had tried to track the animal responsible for destroying their livestock. "Why has no-one tried to track or hunt the animal down?"

Estoup's eyes dulled and his mouth tightened. The farmer reached out for the bottle to refill his wine glass. Gadret noticed that the old man's hands trembled as he put the glass to his mouth and gulped down the wine, "Because the same Beast took the Boussé girl."

\* \* \*

Daniel Abrages actually looked relieved when Maury and his gendarme knocked on the door, and he gladly accepted their invitation to the gendarmerie. "I thought you'd be back," he said.

\* \* \*

"Genevieve Boussé you say?" Gadret could almost hear the professor's mind casting itself back. "Yes, I think I remember." Sanchez said, "She went missing several years ago from a farm near Espadrels."

Good - thought Gadret, who had not mentioned the name of the village.

The Professor went on, "She was fifteen or sixteen years old, I think I'm right in saying that she had Down's syndrome or some other type of learning disability. Her parents were farm workers. No-one actually saw her disappear, yet villagers were convinced that she was taken by the Beast."

Gadret took notes as the professor went on, "The police investigators at that time did not take the beast theory seriously, I think they treated the case as a straightforward missing persons."

"Did you know that the farmers around Espadrels had a spate of livestock attacks around the same time?" asked Gadret.

"I can't remember reading or hearing anything about those," said Sanchez.

"It's not likely that you did, apparently the villagers thought the Beast was taking retribution against them for saying it took the girl."

Sanchez tutted, "People are still very superstitious about the Beast in the remotest areas of Lozère."

* * *

"Am I being arrested?" asked Abrages, as they entered the gendarmerie.

"You are here for questioning." Maury replied. "But you will be cautioned and securely held until that interview has taken place. Do you want a lawyer present?"

"I don't need one." Abrages stated.

* * *

Gadret's next phone call was to Maury.

"I remember the case well," said the inspector, "My old boss Carnot led the investigation. He was convinced that the girl ran away from her parents, apparently they were keeping her under lock and key, weren't letting her go to school or outside. Some of her belongings were gone, there was no sign of forced entry and no one had seen anything. The parents kept on about a beast lurking nearby in the woods for a couple of weeks before she disappeared."

"Others in the village mentioned seeing the beast too and before anyone knew it the Bête du Gevaudan had become responsible. I remember Carnot getting really frustrated; he couldn't figure how the girl could have disappeared so completely without someone else's help. He felt that there was somebody in the village who knew exactly what had happened, but who was keeping it secret."

"Is it worth me digging around a bit more while I'm here?" Gadret asked.

"No, I don't think so," replied the inspector, "Get yourself home, I want you to come into the office tomorrow morning. I've got Daniel Abrages here, in a holding cell, we need to process him together."

As Gadret rang off, there was tapping on the glass of the car's door, a dark shape loomed and a face pressed itself to the windscreen. The sergeant was surprised to see it was old Estoup, his eyes anxious in his lined face. He wound down the window.

"People always said that the Soula's knew more about what happened to the Boussé girl than they let on," the old man blurted out.

"The Soulas? Where can I find them?" asked Gadret.

Estoup's eyes rolled, in the mirror Gadret noticed a tractor moving along the lane towards them. "I've said too much already!" the old farmer said cryptically, "Goodbye sergeant."

As he drove out of the village Gadret caught sight of an old ivy-covered letterbox at the end of a lane, half hidden by overgrowth. He stopped the car and looked at it, 'Soula' it said, written in permanent marker on its lid.

He drove the car along a little used track that climbed away from the village and into the pines. A slate roof appeared, under a smoking chimney, then grey walls. The farmhouse was ramshackle; a lean-to housed an old wartime Willy's Jeep and an equally ancient tractor. Pecking chickens took flight as Gadret's Renault edged into in the yard and the curtains twitched.

* * *

Danczjac laid his hand softly on the dozing Platigny's shoulder and whispered, "The wolves are nearly here."

The officer passed the naturalist binoculars and pointed down the steep-sided valley. Presently the three wolves came into view, padding along in single file, at their head a strong young male. Laura could see nothing of the legionnaires who sat in ambush, yet the wolves seemed wary as they continued towards the col.

Just before leaving the cover of tufts of broom and entering the firing zone they halted, the young male's muzzle raised to sniff at the air.

Movement behind the wolves caught Platigny's eye, two heavily camouflaged legionnaires broke cover just two hundred metres behind the animals. This prompted the wolves forward at a trot into the carefully laid ambush. Danczjac spoke an order into his microphone and a volley of shots rang out.

The wolves momentarily faltered then continued forward, but they were slowing on unsteady legs. Presently they succumbed one by one to the tranquillising effect of the darts and keeled to their sides on the hillside.

* * *

A figure came to the doorway as Gadret alighted from the car, black eyes looked at him from a white-moustachioed, dark and wrinkly visage.

Gadret introduced himself, the blue clad man nodded, "I expect you've come about the Beast," he said.

Gadret nodded, "I understand you can tell me something about the disappearance of Genevieve Boussé."

The man shook his head, "No."

"But you can tell me something about the beast?"

"Better," said the man, "I can show you its lair." He turned back into the house.

"Get into the Jeep," he called, "I will get the guns."

Gadret turned back to the police car and reached for his pistol and shoulder holster under the front seat.

The man re-emerged carrying two rifles and looked scornfully at the sergeant's handgun. "You're better off with one of these!" he said throwing a rifle to the policeman. It was a high velocity hunting rifle with scope. "I am Soula, by the way," said the man holding out a clip of ammunition.

"Its lair is some way into the mountain." Soula said, walking toward the Willys. "You are a good shot aren't you? I'd have hunted the thing by myself before now but my eyes aren't what they used to be."

Gadret nodded, "A marksman."

"Good!" said Soula, pressing the starter and gunning the old Jeep into life.

* * *

Laura checked the sedated wolves over carefully; they were all in amazing condition, much sleeker and fitter than those in the wolf-park. The tattoos confirmed that the wolves were three of the escapees.

One of the Russian trackers came across to the naturalist, "These are like the wolves in Siberia," he said in thickly accented French.

Laura nodded, "Yes, they were bred from Siberian wolves."

The soldier smiled, and the two stood side-by-side looking over the wolves in silent admiration.

"Wolves like this do not attack people," said the soldier.

* * *

The phone rang. "Maury?" Queried a female voice on a very echoing line.

"Yes," Said the inspector recognising the voice, "Is that you Doctor Platigny?"

"Hello, inspector we captured three wolves about twenty minutes ago..." Laura was shouting over a roaring background. "I can confirm that they are all from Marvejols. We are returning them there now."

"Three you say?"

"Yes!"

"Then we need to account for another three."

The line crackled and Platigny's voice was faraway and indistinct.

"Allo? Allo Doctor?"

Laura's voice came back stronger, "Allo Inspector. I was just asking the trackers if they think we missed any, they are adamant that we have not...Did you say three need accounting for?"

"Yes," replied the Maury. "Gadret tracked down two, so we are three missing."

"In what sort of condition are the two Gadret found?" asked the naturalist.

"I'm afraid they are dead Doctor Platigny, I'm sorry."

"They were definitely Marvejols wolves?"

"Yes, their identity numbers tally."

Laura fell silent and Maury could now readily identify the background roar as helicopter engines. "Doctor?"

"I'm still here inspector."

"Get yourself and your wolves back home, I will have details of the two dead wolves emailed to you at the Wolf Park, get some rest, then come in and see me tomorrow."

* * *

From the filing cabinet Maury retrieved Fabienne Sonnester's dossier, as he went through the file his mind went to the girl's poor parents and their anguish at not knowing what had become of her. Perhaps the man downstairs in the holding cell may yet have the answers that they so desired.

He put on his raincoat, time for some good old-fashioned door to door, he thought. Someone somewhere knew what had happened to Enrik Rrukaj, Rue Hotchkiss was just a ten-minute walk away.

* * *

Soula drove the Jeep expertly up the forest track that led from his house into the massif. The track was rutted and rocky and the old farmer wrestled the bucking machine through the stunted trees. His concentration and the constant movement of the Jeep made conversation impossible. So Gadret cradled the rifle and hung tight onto a convenient handhold.

* * *

Rue Hotchkiss was a quiet and neglected road leading to allotments. The houses were characterless, with grey concrete render and red-oxide ironwork.

A peculiar smell wafted on the damp air, Maury tried to place it as he rang the doorbell to number 45bis, he didn't expect a reply and so was surprised when a dark eye looked him up and down as the door opened a centimetre.

Maury waved his identity card and explained his business. The door opened onto a wiry man in his thirties who tried vainly to disguise his premature baldness with a straggly comb over.

"Come in," the man said with a thick east European accent.

As he stepped into the doorway Maury placed the smell - coriander. The scent grew stronger as he was led into the house. He was ushered into a tiny kitchen and shown into a rickety chair at the messy table.

The wiry man cleared the table top with shaking hands as he spoke haltingly in bad French, "Rrukaj and me, we worked in the forest. We worked black, I cannot tell you who employed us, but he was fair and

94

we both have families to feed. Enrik stacked the wood I was cutting with the chainsaw; we worked together as a team. We stopped for a break; he went to answer a call of nature in the forest. About ten minutes later I heard him cry out. I went to look for him, but he was not there. I called others who were working nearby, they were Algerians, and we looked together. We found blood on the side of a tree but nothing of Rrukaj. We were frightened. Then, one of the Algerians said he saw something moving behind the trees. I looked and saw something big with grey fur going behind a rock. We ran back into the clearing and found the boss. We got our things and we haven't worked in that part of the forest since.

"I wanted to tell the police, but that would have meant trouble for everyone, so we said nothing. The boss said it was the Beast and that there was nothing anyone could do for Enrik, he was probably dead anyway. I did what I could for Enrik's family. I phoned his brother and he came from Germany to collect them."

Maury pulled a map from his raincoat pocket, "Do you think you could show me where this happened?" he asked, as he unfolded it on the table.

The man pored over the map his finger tracing a route north-eastward from Mende.

"Around here," he said, his finger indicating a forested area near the isolated hamlet of Les Salesses, about forty kilometres south of Pradelles where the unfortunate Descartes had disappeared while fishing on the Lac de Boucher.

* * *

At last Soula brought the machine to a stop, the track had petered out into little more than rough ground between silver birches. "We've got to walk from here," he said.

Gadret alighted, stretched and looked around him at the bleak wilderness while the farmer picked up his own rifle, loaded and cocked it.

"I'm sorry sergeant," he said quietly as he brought its stock to his shoulder, aimed straight at the policeman and squeezed the trigger.

The impact of the bullet span Gadret around and he fell into a clump of ferns. Disoriented and with ears ringing the wounded sergeant obeyed instinct and training by rolling away into the under-brush. He was aware that his breathing was ragged, with his left hand he reached across to find the small entry wound in the right side of his chest.

Soula was coming around the Jeep, expelling the spent casing and cocking a new round into the breach. Suspecting that the rifle he was still clutching might not fire Gadret discarded it and pulled his service pistol from the holster. The farmer came closer, his eyes looking for the wounded policeman amongst the undergrowth.

Gadret did not hesitate; he emptied his semi-automatic at Soula, half expecting to be shot again. The old man slowly fell to his knees and was prevented from falling forward by the rifle that now acted as a prop for his lifeless body; he simply knelt there like a supplicant while his blood drained from holes in his riddled chest.

Gadret, aware that his own life was ebbing away with the blood that bubbled from his chest cavity and filled his mouth, felt for his mobile phone. He cursed inwardly when he saw that he had no network coverage. Somehow he had to help himself, he'd noticed old plastic fertilizer bags in the back of the jeep, and he staggered past Soula and got one. He wrapped it tightly about his torso hoping to prevent his lung from fully collapsing. The key hung in the Jeep's ignition; he pulled himself behind the wheel and started the engine.

Fifty minutes later, pain-wracked and drifting into semi-consciousness Gadret arrived in Soula's farmyard. He was relieved to find that his mobile phone at last had access to the network and was able to summon assistance before allowing himself to close his eyes.

* * *

Maury never reached the woodland where he'd hoped to retrieve clues on Rrukaj's sudden disappearance. The car radio crackled and he was summoned to return as a matter of urgency to Mende's gendarmerie where a helicopter was awaiting him on the landing-pad.

"What's the emergency?" he asked, reluctant to turn the car around so close to his objective.

"Sergeant Gadret has been shot!" came the reply.

As Maury stepped from the helicopter, paramedics were carrying Gadret, on a stretcher, towards the aircraft. The inspector went over to the stricken sergeant, to find him unconscious and attached to various pipes and tubes, including a ventilator.

He caught the eye of one of the medics, "Will he be okay?" he asked.

The medic's face was impassive, "It's touch and go."

They passed by and started strapping the sergeant into the dark blue fuselage. Then, the doors slammed and the engines started screaming with power, sending a swirling typhoon of dust across the farmyard.

Maury was blown before it into the path of three local gendarmes who were standing by Soula's Jeep awaiting instructions; Maury directed two of them to take their own four-wheel drive car up the track to guard Soula's body.

He decided he would begin in the farmhouse and directed the remaining gendarme to examine the outbuildings. He passed close to the ancient Jeep, noticing the blood smearing the swabs of its bucket seats. What had Gadret stumbled upon, why had he been shot by an old farmer?

The farm's interior was gloomy, the furnishings rough, simple and devoid of any conveniences or comforts. On the television were black and white photographs in cheap frames, memoirs of the Soula's family life: pictures of a middle-aged couple and their child; of a little, rotund and smiling boy sitting on his father's lap at the wheel of the Willy's; of

97

an erect farmer and his frail looking wife; of the same farmer and a well-built youth in mourning suits and the ubiquitous picture of children ranked in anonymous formal rows for their school photograph.

The remaining local gendarme entered and thrust something at Maury, the inspector looked down at a dog-eared notebook. "Sergeant Gadret's notebook inspector, I found it in his car."

Maury looked carefully at the gendarme's face and smiled, "It's Lalande isn't it? It's been a long time," he said offering his hand in greeting.

* * *

"According to this notebook sergeant Gadret called here today."

Estoup nodded.

"Did he talk to you about the Beast?" Maury asked.

"Yes, he did," confirmed the old man.

"What did you tell him?"

"I told him just what it says there in that book you read out!"

"You told him about Genevieve Boussé's disappearance too."

"I mentioned it."

"Did you tell him that Soula might be able to help him?"

"I mentioned that Soula had livestock taken by some sort of animal too."

"Thank you, Monsieur Estoup," said Maury wondering why the old man was lying.

He thanked the farmer for his time and returned to Gadret's car where Lalande sat waiting for him.

"Where now Inspector?" the gendarme asked.

Lalande had worked with Maury when the Boussé girl went missing. "Take me to the Boussé place will you?" he directed.

The gendarme's brow furrowed, "But the family left years ago inspector. You'll find nothing there."

"There may still be ghosts," said Maury, putting on his seatbelt.

* * *

The Boussé farm was ramshackle and neglected, although the barns were still used by neighbouring farmers for the storage of big bales of hay and straw. The house still seemed solid except for a collapsed gutter and a downpipe swinging dangerously from one corner. Maury tried the front-door handle, which squeaked ineffectually, while Lalande walked towards the lean-to shed cum garage that sheltered a side door into the kitchen.

Soon Maury heard Lalande's footsteps crunching and loud upon the bare stone floor and the metallic clack of the lock as the front door was opened. Maury stepped inside, his eyes adjusting to the gloom.

Something crunched and cracked under his feet, looking down the floor appeared black, until Maury realised that it was covered with a uniform layer of dead flies. He moved cautiously to the kitchen and looked around.

The fireplace now cold and sooty-black was washed in dappled light revealing the obligatory photographs of the family arranged on the mantle above. Maury, blew the dust from the largest, revealing a school photo identical to that in the Soula house.

* * *

Back in Soula's farmhouse Maury picked up the picture frame from the mantle and turned it around; unlike the Boussé photo - which had been glued into position - this one was mounted with old gummed tape. Maury reached into his pocket for his pocketknife and carefully cut through the tape to free the photograph.

As expected on the back there was a list of student names, left to right, front to back. Genevieve Boussé was in the centre of the front row. The inspector's eyes scanned the remaining names until he saw the surname Soula - Hercules Soula was standing second from left on the back row. Turning the frame around he recognised the sturdy youth he assumed must be Soula's son.

* * *

Standing in the dimly lit corridor on a floor so polished that it almost looked liquid, Maury watched the rise and fall of Gadret's chest. Of the sergeant himself the inspector hardly recognised anything, a mask covered his face and he lay angled on a bed surrounded by screens and monitors that whirred and flashed sequentially. Tubes and lines entered Gadret's body under bright white gauzes, from the machines.

Maury watched the hypnotic rhythm that indicated that the inert form of his colleague was alive and rang Laura Platigny's number. A soft female voice answered.

"Hello, Doctor Platigny, this is inspector Maury speaking, I hope I haven't called at an inconvenient time.

"I'm calling from the hospital in Mende, there's been an incident, perhaps you have seen the news..."

Maury looked down the corridor to his left where a nurse sat at her workstation filling in forms, her uniform luminous under the glare of a desktop lamp.

"Well, the policeman concerned is sergeant Gadret. The doctors say that he is in a very serious but stable condition..."

"No, I'm not sure what that means.  As far as I can ascertain from the doctors, it means that Gadret is in an induced coma and that they worked on haemorrhaging to internal organs."

"He was visiting a farm in the village of Espradels...e-s-p-r-a-d-e-l-s, in the commune of Luc / Cheylard-l'Eveque."

"Yes, I'm sure Gadret was on to something...I have some leads to follow, but I wondered if it would be worth looking in the area for your missing wolves... When it is convenient for you, I don't think there is any rush...Will you need any gendarmes?... Okay, fair enough...Goodnight doctor and thank you."

He flipped the mobile phone shut, and looking back through the window at his wounded colleague he caught sight of his own reflection in the glass. He straightened his collar and turned towards the double doors at the end of the corridor.

"Inspector Maury?" Asked an immaculately dressed middle aged nurse. She sat stationed in an alcove by the door and held out the receiver of the large old-fashioned telephone on her desk.

Maury nodded and took the receiver, "Allo."

The professor sounded excited, "Inspector. This is Sanchez, I need to see you urgently."

"Tomorrow?"

"Sooner."

"Now?"

"That would be fine, I'll be expecting you." Sanchez said as he hung up.

* * *

Sanchez was right, the pattern of the pins in the map showed that the majority of attacks in the past sixteen years were taking place in certain areas according to the seasons.

In spring attacks took place in the north-west quadrant of a circle radiating from the northern slopes of Mont Lozère, summer attacks took place in the north-east, autumn attacks in the south-east and winter attacks in the south west.

At, or very near the centre was Espadrels.

* * *

As she lay in bed listening to the inevitable rainstorm patter against the shutters, Laura wondered about the fate of the three wolves that were still unaccounted for. What had become of them?

The wolves were all three young females. Vast tracts of land and mountain ranges separated the Marvejols wolves from their Spanish, Italian and Eastern European cousins. The only hope that there may be was that there had been a dispersal, a natural splitting of the pack with one or two of the missing wolves attempting to reach other wolf populations by themselves. Lone female wolves such as OR7 in the United States and Pluie in Canada had travelled vast distances alone, OR7 had covered        nearly 2000 kilometres, from Oregon to California in just 42 days.    Alone, wolves managed to pass by un-noticed, to shake off their pursuers and successfully survive.

Much as she hoped that they were alive and thriving – it was more likely that they were dead.


As the Siberian legionnaire had said, it was highly improbable that the wolves were in any case culpable suspects in the disappearance of Fabienne Sonnester, the death of Fausto Claudi or any other human victim.

*D*eciding that a direct assault seemed hopeless, some locals decided upon subterfuge.

One suggested making "artificial women" that would be placed on the edge of the woods in which the Beast was known to lurk. It was very easy: a bag made of ewe's skin would be made up to imitate the body, two other elongated bags would be attached to portray the legs; Finally the figurine would be crowned by a head made from bladder full of blood filled sponges, painted to look realistic, all seasoned quite naturally with arsenic, so that the duped Beast would meet a grisly end.

Another proposed selecting 25 bold men, and to cover them with the skins of lions, bears, leopards, stags, does, calves, goats, wild boars and wolves and with a hat filled with knife blades: each of these costumes would be adorned with a little box containing 12 ounces of Christian fat mixed with viper blood and each man supplied with 3 square bullets previously bitten by a girl...

Another had dreamed up a doomsday machine made up of 30 shotguns that would be triggered by the contortions of a young veal calf upon 30 ropes, set in motion by its struggles in the face of the ravening Beast.

While men schemed, the Beast continued wreaking havoc and its boldness seemed to increase.

Around January 15th, it snatched a 14 year-old boy, Jean Chateauneuf, from the parish of Crezes. The next day, as the boy's distraught father was crying in his kitchen, the Beast looked in upon him by the window, putting its legs on the windowsill.

On February 2nd, it crossed the village of Saint-Amant at a jog while the villagers were attending Mass; unsuccessfully trying to break and enter the houses in order to find children but all doors were closed and it ran away, vexed.

September 5

People disappearing without trace, wolf hairs and human remains littered deep in the forest far from where they'd disappeared. Yes, thought Maury, this case was very strange.

But whatever dark secrets were hidden by Fabienne Sonnester, he was sure now that they had no bearing on her disappearance. The link to Dortmund could surely only be circumstantial.

Maury felt that maybe they were overlooking something vital and thought once again about the victims: two students from Germany, a local civil servant and an Albanian wood cutter, all somehow connected with the secretive community of Espradels and the two farming families of the Boussés and the Soulas.

What then could be the motives for these disappearances and killings? What had they in common apart from their epicentre?

They were getting close to the truth; Gadret's unfortunate shooting had proven that. It was a shame that the only person who could definitely have helped them, old Soula, had been shot and killed by the Sergeant.

Never mind, thought Maury, that will not put me off. I am a policeman, I ask questions.

* * *

Laura woke, pulled the duvet from her face and looked at the clock on her bedside table. The red digits indicated 05:46. She snuggled back under the covers for a few moments then with an effort extracted herself from her cosy bedding. She sat swaying on the edge of the bed for a moment, her long legs before her as a counterbalance and stretched wide with a yawn, then she rose and padded towards the en-suite shower.

After the invigoration of the hot water she padded naked back into the bedroom, her hair up in a white towel, and rifled through her drawers for clothes, then pulled herself into sports underwear and a tracksuit, put her day clothes into a rucksack and finally laced on her running shoes.

Pausing only to grab a couple of litre bottles of mineral water and a banana, she locked the door to her cottage and stowed her things on the back seat of her Land-rover. By the dull glow of the interior light she grabbed her Michelin motoring atlas and plotted a route to Espadrels. She rubbed most of the moisture out of her hair with the towel then threw it onto the back seat alongside her other things and started the engine.

* * *

Maury slipped out of the house early and went to his office where the thin folder on Soula awaited him.

The man had inherited the farm, on which he'd been born, from his father, he had served as a conscript in Algeria where he'd served with distinction. He'd married and with his wife had just the one son - Hercules. Soula's wife had died while Hercules was still at school in Mende. He'd been the sole occupant of the farm according to the past censuses, had made ends meet by mixed farming and forestry, was debt free and had no criminal record whatever. There was no history of mental illness and he was in rude health.

However, he'd shot a policeman simply because he'd turned up on the doorstep...

Espradels was probably not a safe place to be until Gadret had given his statement.

Maury sent a text to Laura Platigny to tell her to forgo her visit to the village to look for wolves, he then telephoned Sanchez and was surprised to get the professor rather than his answerphone.

"I'd like to go over things again Professor Sanchez. Can you come by the gendarmerie when it's convenient?"

* * *

Parking her car at the entrance to the village Laura pulled the hair severely back from her face and captured her ponytail in a tight hairband. Then she drank half the contents of one of her water bottles, grabbed a compass from the glove-box and jumped out into the morning chill.

She stretched for several minutes before trotting uphill away from the car towards the looming village buildings. Her muscular tightness eased as she passed along the tarmac ribbon that snaked through the houses.

Somewhere a dog barked and there was the hum of idling machinery. She headed east toward the brightening sky, and then forked right onto a track that ran along the flank of the mountain. Presently the surface deteriorated into muddy single-track with boulders like grey stepping-stones at random spacings and angles along its length. Laura concentrated hard on placing her feet as she ran, careful to ensure that she would not turn an ankle or trip headlong. After several undulating kilometres the path re-joined a road and descended in tight switchbacks toward a ruined castle.

Sweating, Laura forked away from the ruin and started to make her return journey by running cross-country, she pushed uphill towards a ridge as the sun threw its first watery rays across the steely sky.

At the ridge she stopped and took in her surroundings from its high vantage point, her breath rasping in the cold air. Cloud hung in the valleys and swirled slowly over the forested slopes of the massif. Here and there rays of yellow sunlight lit up sections of the mountains, throwing dark treetops and golden ferns into contrast. Her eyes rolled across the rugged landscape searching for any sign of wolves.

She checked her compass bearings and started running west along the ridge figuring that it would bring her to within a kilometre of Espadrels. The going was difficult and Laura had to concentrate hard on the terrain before her, but as she crested a rise, that gave her a better view of the surrounding slopes, she stopped and looked carefully around. Something pale against the dark tree line about three hundred metres away caught her eye.

The indistinct form was moving, something flapping as if in a breeze, which struck her as strange when the air was relatively still. Mystified, Laura continued looking at the object until with a gasp she recognised what she was seeing - it was a naked child, arm flapping as it sat at the base of the pines.

What was a naked child doing sat at the edge of a forest in this wilderness? Laura wondered. Was it accompanied, its parent camping or working nearby?

Then something else moved in the trees behind the child - indistinct, grey-brown - Laura's heart leapt - something large and sinuous was edging toward the playing infant.

Laura wanted to cry a warning, but was shocked into silence when the child rose on its unsteady legs and toddled into the trees towards the half-hidden beast.

Laura felt her imagination must have been playing tricks, now there was no sign of anything in the tree line; she wanted to dismiss what she'd seen as a figment of her imagination. Perhaps a fleeting spot of bright sunshine had illuminated something against the dark of the forest?

Yet, the hairs on Laura's neck stood on end and a real sense of fear overtook her.

A glimpse of fast-moving grey flickering through the trees trunks on a course parallel to her own convinced her to turn on her heel and run. She ran as she'd never run before, fuelled by adrenalin she leapt over boulders and crashed through brambles, oblivious of their dangers, until at last the roofs of Espadrels came into view. Only then, did Laura dare to look behind her. Panting, she cast her eyes along the ridge but there was nothing to see on the path that she had taken. But within the forest of thickly grown pines one hundred meters away a grey-brown form sank back into the darkness between the trees.

Back in the sanctuary of her Land Rover Laura gripped the steering wheel tightly in order to steady the violent waves of trembling that coursed through her body. Once composed, she reached for her fleece jacket and pulled it around her shoulders.

Looking out at the peaceful village through the windscreen she wondered if perhaps she had been imagining the naked infant on the tree line and the dark presence that pursued her headlong rush back to the car. Hesitantly she reached for her mobile phone then scrolled until she found Maury's number.

The phone beeped to indicate that a message had been received - words filled the screen: "Do not go to Espadrels. Please ring me. Maury."

"Inspector? Allo...It's Laura Platigny...I'm afraid I got your message too late..." Laura began sobbing.

Maury's voice was clear and calm, "Where are you Laura? Are you in Espadrels? Are you safe?"

Laura managed to compose herself, "Yes, I am safe."

"Good. Where are you exactly?"

"I am in my car near the village."

"I...I saw something." Laura stammered.

* * *

"You were quite right professor, Espadrels does seem to be at the centre of our mystery. Yesterday sergeant Gadret was shot while conducting enquiries in the area, this morning Doctor Platigny was involved in an incident on the outskirts of the village." Maury looked at Sanchez to monitor his reaction.

Sanchez seemed unsurprised, "There is good cover in the woodlands

108

above Espadrels, it would be a good place for a predator to winter."

Maury grunted, "So you are still convinced that the Beast exists?"

"Why not? There are a lot of collaborating reports to support the theory." Sanchez said patting a thick file on the desk.

Maury sat back in his chair and scratched at his chin, "So what would you do now, if you were in my shoes Professor?"

Sanchez tapped the file, "If sergeant Gadret or doctor Platigny witnessed a large grey-brown animal, I would suggest that you put your expert legionnaire trackers in the area." He looked at the policeman for reaction.

Maury nodded slightly, "The legionnaires are on their way. What else would you do in my place Professor?"

"We must ask why it is that Gadret was shot in the course of his investigations."

"He was shot by a local farmer called Soula."

"Soula? I can't say I've ever heard that name."

"He seems to be connected to the Boussé affair."

"The Boussé girl's disappearance! Surely not, not after so many years. It is surely just a coincidence?"

Maury looked directly at Sanchez, his eyes humourless and unblinking, "I don't believe in coincidence."

* * *

"So we meet again doctor." Said the smiling Danczjac, offering his hand to Laura. "Are you up to this? I hear you had quite a fright this morning."

"I'm okay lieutenant," Laura smiled at the Siberian standing behind the officer, the same man who didn't think that wolves were responsible for the mysterious disappearances in the region. He smiled and nodded in acknowledgement.

"Inspector Maury has given us orders to accompany you to the site of your 'incident', the corporal and I will then search the area." Said Danczjac, picking up his backpack and rifle, he gestured towards Espadrels, "Please lead on."

* * *

The school was as quiet as he remembered.

The school secretary seemed surprised to see Maury again, "You wish to see Madame Tournant?"

Maury nodded, "Yes please."

After checking that the headmistress was free, the secretary signalled Maury into her office.

Although she looked a little puzzled, there was a hint of pleasure at the corners of her mouth and a sparkle in her eye as Madame Tournant removed her glasses and motioned the detective towards a chair, "Inspector Maury, it is a pleasure to see you, how can I help you this morning. It cannot be about the Rrukaj girl can it, I hear that you tracked her down?"

Maury placed a heavy duty buff envelope on the desk in front of the teacher, "Could you tell me anything about some children in this photo?"

Delicately and without hurry, Madame Tournant replaced her bi-focal glasses on the bridge of her narrow nose and slid the black and white photo from the envelope.

"This is very old," she said. She then pored over the photograph carefully, turning it to look at the information on the back. She pursed her lips, "This was taken at the Roman Catholic Special Needs school in Mende before it closed. The date is smudged. The school has gone now, all the children now come here...This is well before my time."

"Who would remember these children?" asked Maury.

"No-one who presently teaches here would remember them."

"So you cannot help me?"

"Did I say that Inspector?" Madame Tournant's tone was mocking, almost flirtatious. "We have the old school records here in the archive."

"Could I see them?"

Reaching into an open desk drawer the head teacher lifted a bunch of bronze keys, stood, smoothed down her pencil skirt and turned neatly on a shapely nylon-clad ankle picking up the photo from her desk as she turned, "Follow me inspector," she directed.

Maury followed her shapely form, watching its wiggle, as she led him down the corridor to the archive, unlocked its substantial modern locks and switched on the lights. Finely manicured hands waved over uniform grey filing cabinets, clearly marked with academic year dates, as she walked into the sombre and stale smelling archive, "The records in these are modern, the records we need to look at will be at the back."

She pressed on into the room that Maury could now see was quite large, with each wall lined with cabinets and more in an island of two rows in its centre. Stopping at a cabinet well into the room Madame Tournant placed the photograph from the Soula farm face up on its top, pulled open a middle drawer and extracted one of the fat yellow folders it contained.

The folder was secured by a string, which the teacher's nimble fingers had soon unknotted. Reaching into the front of the folder she pulled out a wad of photographs. "One of these should match yours," she said, halving the wad and passing half to Maury.

With the Soula photograph on top of the filing cabinet before them, they compared the photographs. They seemed identical, the children all stood in uniform rows flanked by unsmiling teachers, eyes fixed, staring at the glass lens of the large format camera that took these

111

high definition black and white images.

Maury was relieved when the head teacher exclaimed, "Ah! I think this is it."

She placed the two photos side by side and, apart from condition, they were identical. "Now, if we turn this one over we should find the date."

Sure enough, a franked stamp on the archived copy gave the year.

Now Madame Tournant extracted a second yellow folder and extracted a list of names, "These people were on the staff of the Roman Catholic school at the time." She placed it next to the photograph, dug deeper into the folder and extracted a further typewritten and stapled list of names, "And this list should be of the students."

"Which children interest you?"

"There are two: Boussé, Genevieve and Soula, Hercules."

\* \* \*

"Here...I was about here," said Laura looking down at the pathway and across at the mountainside to get her bearings.

"You are sure?" asked Danczjac.

Laura nodded.

The lieutenant set up a tripod in front of her. "Where on the hillside did you see the child?" he asked, as he ensured the apparatus was stable.

Laura pointed to where she saw the child, she was not certain that it had been a child she had seen, now that the soldier was taking her story seriously, but the spot was quite distinct.

Danczjac fixed a sighting device on the tripod. "Find the spot by looking through this," he instructed.

Laura put her eye to the strange device. The scene, at first blurred, came into sudden and sharp focus. She swung the lens from side to side to orient herself then picked out the spot on the treeline where she had seen the apparition.

"Can you centre the cross-hairs on the exact spot?" asked Danczjac pressing a button that brought fine cross-hairs dancing across the viewfinder. "Tell me when."

She made a few fine adjustments, "Now," said Laura.

Danczjac pressed another button that seemed to do nothing. Laura looked up from the eyepiece as the Lieutenant spoke instructions in Russian into his handheld radio. He pointed to a small cylindrical attachment under the viewfinder. "This emits a beam that paints the target," he explained.

Looking at her expression he explained in other terms, "This fires a beam at the area you aimed for. My men have special equipment that allows them to find the area where it is falling."

As Laura and the Lieutenant watched, two legionnaires moved uphill toward the treeline. Presently the radio crackled and Danczjac gave instructions to his men. For Laura's benefit he pointed towards them, "They are in the area now. I have told them to enter the trees and look for anything that seems out of place."

Laura watched the soldiers carefully quartering the ground where, just a few short hours ago, she had seen the naked child. Then they disappeared among the trees. Some minutes later, the radio once again came to life. Danczjac turned to Laura, "Can you direct the beam to where you saw the animal in the trees?"

* * *

"So, this Madame Perrion is she still around?" Maury asked.

Madame Tournant had picked the name from a list of teachers that had taught both the Soula and Boussé children. She looked at him over

113

her bi-focals, "Thirty years ago Elizabeth Perrion was my mentor when I first entered teaching."

Maury didn't know what to say. Like many schoolteachers, Madame Tournant's age was indeterminate.

A smile touched the corners of the head teacher's mouth, "Are you trying to calculate how old she must be Inspector?" she asked, with a hint of coquettishness.

"Shall I give you a clue?" her eyes sparkled with mischief, "I know that she is exactly thirty years older than I am."

Maury remained silent, but the laughing eyes challenged him and he made a reluctant guess. "She must be around seventy," he proffered, hoping that he would not give offence.

"You are some way out inspector," Madame Tournant purred, "She is eighty-one on the twenty-third of March."

"It may interest you to know that I am still in contact with Madame Perrion," said Madame Tournant, returning to her business-like self. "She lives on her family farm near Lagrasse on the edge of the Corbières in Aude."

"Do you have contact details?" asked Maury.

Madame Tournant shook her head, almost imperceptibly. "I can get the details." The head teacher removed her glasses and regarded Maury with her bright blue eyes. "I presume you need Elizabeth to give you some information about these two ex-pupils?"

"Yes," Maury confirmed.

Still keeping her eyes on Maury's face, Madame Tournant continued, "Elizabeth is profoundly deaf, you would need to ensure that you send officers who can sign."

"I suppose," Maury conceded, wondering where the conversation was going.

"Tomorrow is Saturday. If you want, I could accompany you to see her, I could sign for you. She would be at ease with a policeman in my company."

Maury was taken aback, but looking at Madame Tournant's pretty face he could see the plan had advantages.

She must have read assent in his look, the headmistress smiled. "It's a bit of a drive. Pick me up early, let's say seven from my apartment. I will give you the address in a moment...And please, call me Belle."

* * *

The legionnaires returned from quartering the areas that Laura had 'painted'. They shook their heads, they had nothing to report, Danczjac turned to Laura and shrugged.

"Could you take me over there?" asked Laura.

Danczjac nodded and directed one of the recently returned legionnaires to accompany Laura to the far hillside.

Once at the place where Laura had identified the naked child they stopped. Laura asked the soldier for his field glasses and looked around. There was no sign of the village from this viewpoint, but about two kilometres away the gable end of a farmhouse nestling among trees could be seen. Laura got her large scale map from her pocket and plotted the farmhouse's position. It was the Soula farm.

* * *

The uniformed gendarme started the recorder, a handcuffed and frail-looking Abrages sat opposite an equally exhausted Maury.

Maury passed some movie stills over the table, "There were several pornographic videos on the hard-drive of your computer. These are stills from one you downloaded from the Eurorevenue site in Germany in June. Is that right?"

"Yes."

"Let the record show Exhibits A, B, C and D. Do you recognise the blonde girl in these pictures?"

"No. She's wearing a mask."

"Could this be the girl you saw at the camp-site?"

"The camp-site at the gorge?" Abrages looked dismayed.

"Is it?" Maury slid over another set of photographs, "Do you recognise the girl in these?" he asked.

"Yes. Is it the same girl?"

"Let the record show that the witness recognises Fabienne Sonnester from Exhibits E, F, G and H."

"What was this girl doing when you saw her?"

"Sunbathing, and reading a book."

"What book?"

"I couldn't see."

"Can you describe what she was wearing?"

A pause..."She wasn't wearing anything."

"She was naked?"

"Yes. That's how I recognised her from the pictures."

At Maury's puzzled expression, Abrages leant over pointed at the pictures and explained, "She had that same little tattoo on her shoulder, a little dolphin..."

"Ah! Yes, " said Maury, who had supposed the mark to be a mole.

"Did you approach her or communicate with her in any way?"

"No."

"Did you see her boyfriend?"

"No, but I knew he was there...in the tent, she kept talking to him."

"What were they talking about."

"I don't know, it was some foreign language, German I suppose."

"Did they sound angry?"

"No, they spoke quietly to each other."

"So you carried on down to the ravine to fish?"

"Yes."

"You caught three salmon?"

"Yes."

"You definitely didn't recognise the girl from the pornographic film?"

"No...it's just coincidence." Daniel Abrages looked frightened and Maury was inclined to believe him.

"Did you see her again."

A hesitation, "No...I would have liked to, but I didn't."

* * *

He stood once again in the squeaky clean corridor looking at the recumbent figure attached to a tangle of tubes and wires. Gadret's chest rose and fell regularly, lights blinked and mechanisms clicked, their sound echoing faintly.

A dark-uniformed nurse arose from her desk and padded softly to Maury's side clutching a clipboard to her breast. "The sergeant is making very good progress inspector, he is young and strong," she said, "He is breathing unaided now, he will probably gain consciousness tomorrow...Shall I call you and let you know?"

"Yes," replied Maury, "Please do."

* * *

Laura rang the gendarmerie on Maury's direct number. It went straight to answering machine. She spoke , as directed, after the beep. "This is

Laura Platigny, I have a message for inspector Maury. The legionnaires conducted a thorough search in the area where I saw the baby and the beast in the trees, near Espadrels. They found nothing – I'm beginning to think that I may have imagined the whole thing...

"I don't know if its significant, but from where the baby and creature were , you can't see anything of the village except the Soula's farmhouse."

*T*he disaster devastating Gevaudan affected the whole of France; news of its exploits were reported in the Parisian newspapers and the Beast was the talk of the bourgeois. Even King Louis XV, himself, despite other concerns, wanted to show solidarity with his subjects and directed his minister to send troops

In accordance with his instructions, Captain Duhamel headquartered in Saint-Chély with a gathering of the most reputable gunmen of the county. Dividing all the men into eight beats; Duhamel offered a reward of six thousand pounds to the person who killed the Beast. Every parish priest was directed to inform the peasantry that salvation was at hand. Unless it came from hell, the monster was sure to succumb. To further reassure the terrorised populace, the lords of Languedoc ordered that the remains of the Beast, when killed, should be exposed to the public.

The eight beats operated from November 20 to 27 without result. But as soon as the troops returned to their billet, the Beast was reported to be in the area of Sainte-Colombe, where it killed 5 girls, a woman and 4 children...

September 6

Belle wondered why she, as a self-content and successful career woman had so eagerly and brazenly volunteered herself to Maury's service. Her uninhibited actions were embarrassing in hindsight, but then the detective interested her. It was not that he was physically attractive or the possessor of animal magnetism, it would be truer to say that he rather projected an aura of unkempt, gone-to-seed sadness about him. However, in that haggard poorly-shaved face the detective possessed the steadiest and most observant eyes of anyone she had ever met.

At home she'd done her research, Maury had once been the Golden Boy of the Police Academy the most promising young detective in the South of France. Somehow his career had stalled, he'd ended up in the backwaters of Lozère, overpassed and bypassed. But his reputation was such that he'd still ended up leading some very difficult and high-profile investigations.

She also learned that he was presently the lead detective in the case of the missing German students and it was in the course of this investigation that their paths had crossed.

Then, as she thought about it, she was able to put her finger on it, her attraction to Maury was like her one to the forgotten child in the corner of the playground, the self-sufficient semi-feral boy that she ached to nurture and care for.

* * *

She was waiting outside on the pavement, a large umbrella protecting her from the light drizzle. Belle got into the car and settled herself silently into her seat. She graced Maury with a small smile as she secured her seatbelt, "Ready." she said.

They drove the first one hundred kilometres in silence, he concentrating on the wet roads, she on the countryside slipping past the windows. With the rain abating the wipers now just beat

120

intermittently on the screen and Belle suggested music.

Maury pointed toward the glove-box, "The radio doesn't work too well, there are CDs in there."

She looked at the cases carefully before choosing a disc with a look of satisfaction and introducing it into the player.

Maury let out a pleased chuckle as the first track began and the sonorous tones of Paolo Conte filled the car. Soon they were singing along together in pigeon Italian to the familiar tunes, "Chips, chips..."

* * *

This morning, the escapee wolves would leave quarantine and be reintroduced to the park's main population. They were in fine condition – a little underweight – and none the worse for their brief taste of liberty.

Laura drove the four-wheel-drive Mercedes to a vantage point where she could oversee their release. On her command the keepers opened the cages and the wolves filed out. The resident wolves looked on as the escapees padded in single file along the perimeter fence-line as if re-inspecting the constraints of their prison.

Would there be a hierarchical struggle Laura wondered – would the escapees re-assimilate or remain as aloof as they now seemed to be; another pack in the park? She ordered her peripatetic keepers to keep a watch.

Damn Maury! Damn Gadret! Damn Fabienne Sonnester! Damn farmers. Damn them all!...thought Laura.

If it weren't for this damned case the escaped wolves may have been the forerunners of a new phase – the re-assimilation of wild wolves into France. As it was, here they were back in the confines of the Marvejols Wolf Park, a gilded cage, but a prison nonetheless.

Then she scolded herself for her selfishness, she knew, she'd seen with her own eyes that something malevolent stalked the hills of Lozère.

121

Who could blame anyone for thinking it may be the wolves? Maury simply had to eliminate them as suspects in his enquiries. And, if she could spin a positive, if the detective eliminated them, perhaps there was hope of wolves once again roaming the Gevaudan.

Above all, Damn you Beast!

* * *

As they travelled south the music and brightening weather lifted their spirits. Belle was easy company and she appeared to be enjoying the role of deejay, selecting favourite tracks from Maury's eclectic music collection.

At last they arrived, in brilliant sunshine, outside a newly-built Spanish style villa on the outskirts of Lagrasse, and they were struck by the fierce heat once they stepped free of the car's air-conditioned interior. Belle turned to Maury, "It may be best for me to have a few minutes with Elizabeth so I can tell her what's going on."

Maury nodded assent and watched as Belle's trim form walked into the Bougainvillea-shaded doorway.

He removed his jacket in the unfamiliar heat, uncomfortably aware that his shirt was un-ironed and removed the tie from his collar.

Presently, Belle beckoned to him from a window, he entered the house and followed the quiet murmur of voices into a large, air-conditioned room with terracotta floor-tiles and sharply modern furniture. He introduced himself to Madame Perrion, a petite and alert elderly woman who sat in an orthopaedic armchair.

She took the photograph he offered and put on the glasses that hung from her neck to examine it, as he sat down in the armchair opposite her. Elizabeth Perrion looked up enquiringly, "What do you need to know Inspector?" she asked, in a clear, precisely articulated voice.

"I want you to tell me all you can about two of the students in that photograph, Genevieve Boussé and Hercules Soula." Maury replied.

Belle rose from her chair, crossed to her old friend and pointed out their faces in the photograph.

A wry smile crossed the old teacher's face. "Ah yes, Genevieve and Hercules...they were sweethearts, the two of them. It was a shame that the Boussé family disapproved of the boy, personally I think they were made for one another.

"They started school together as infants, travelled together on the bus from the same village, sat together in class and played together in the playground. It broke their little hearts when the Boussé family decided to send Genevieve to a special school in Alés when she was fourteen. They thought it would better meet her needs. Of course, it wouldn't have. I heard that when she returned home on holidays the family found her behaviour almost unmanageable. Without her Hercules became very withdrawn, started missing school and then left on his sixteenth birthday to take up a farming job with an uncle near Avignon.

"Both had special needs, they were both elective mutes, he by choice and she because she had a very cleft palate. Hercules was very remedial interested in all things farming but little else. Good with his hands. Liked practical work. She was a little brighter, with Down's Syndrome, very sweet-natured. She practically mothered Hercules, protecting him from bullies, he was big but would never stand up for himself."

"Do you know what happened to them between leaving school and Genevieve's disappearance?" asked Maury.

Madame Perrion watched attentively as Belle signed the detective's question. She nodded in comprehension, "As I say Inspector, Genevieve was placed in the special school near Alés, and Hercules went to work on an uncle's farm near Avignon. She disappeared during her summer vacation back at home in Espradels."

The interview formally over, Maury turned to Belle. "I need to follow up on some of the information Madame Perrion has provided. I have

123

my mobile phone in my car, perhaps you'd like a little time together?"

Belle smiled, "That would be nice," she purred.

"About an hour?"

Again Belle smiled.

Maury took his leave. If he were honest, the research could wait, but the sunshine could not. He'd seen the beckoning brightness from the lounge windows and ached to feel the hot sun on his skin.

At first, the heat's assault was oppressive, but once he'd retrieved the phone from the car and found speckled shelter under a spreading Plane that overlooked a burbling river, he relaxed and mused upon the Sonnester case while watching spotted trout flit upstream in the shadows of the riverbanks. He rang the gendarmerie in Mende, "Release Daniel Abrages without charge, thank him for assisting in our enquiries."

"One more thing. I want all the information that you can find on the Boussé and Soula families from Espradels, particularly on the son Hercules, you may have to get information from Avignon as I understand he went there to work on an uncle's farm after he finished school in Mende."

Maury strolled back towards Madame Perrion's house. Belle saw him from the window and indicated that he should await her in the car. Presently, she sat in the scalding interior that the air conditioning was struggling to cool.

"Isn't this heat nice?" she remarked as she belted-up.

"I'd like to buy you lunch, as a thank you." said Maury.

Belle smiled warmly. "That would be lovely," she said.

Maury pulled the car up to a roadside restaurant with a shady terrace where he and Belle could eat while enjoying the sunshine and heat. The place was quiet and the attentive waiter seemed pleased to see customers, he told them to take a table of their own choosing. Belle opted for a table that enjoyed panoramic views of the vineyards and rugged hillsides of the Corbières. The menu was simple and rustic, Maury quickly decided on the Plat du Jour at the waiter's recommendation and Belle followed suit. While he dithered over what to drink, as a driver, Belle ordered a bottle of the region's finest red, "A glass for you – the rest for me!" she explained.

It really was a pleasant time they passed in each other's company, they relaxed as they ate and watched the world go by. She gently pressed him to talk about himself and he reciprocated. They spoke of childhood, adolescence and their studies with much self-effacing humour and laughter, finding that they had much in common beyond their taste in music. Both were brought up in the countryside; he in Roussillon, she in the Vendée, both went to complete their studies in the city; Maury in Toulouse, Belle in Bordeaux.

Both it seems were good at their jobs, specialists in their respective fields. And both had opted to return from the city to the provincial life.

Now both were middle-aged and contemplating the next phase of their lives, retirement in the sunshine.

More seriously, Belle admitted that she had married badly and had been divorced for eight years. Maury said little of his own marriage but spoke lovingly of his grown up children. She listened attentively and admitted her jealousy and the fact that she had wanted to be a mother.

Too soon, Belle had finished the bottle of wine, Maury two coffees and it was time to return to Lozère.

Sleepily Belle chose a CD of light classical music as Maury drove up out of the sunshine into the overcast of the Causses.

Softly, Maury felt Belle's hand alight on his knee, he looked across at her but she appeared to be asleep in the passenger seat, her head turned to the window. He liked its intimate feel and he left it there as the car thrust into an inevitable wall of drizzle.

Belle woke when the car left the autoroute, she did not remove her hand from Maury's knee until he pulled outside her apartment. "I enjoyed today," she said. "Perhaps we could do it again sometime?"

Maury was tongue-tied, astonished into doing little more than sit as she kissed his cheek and got out of the car. "Call me!" Belle said, turning on a shapely heel and running for the shelter of her doorway.

Maury drove home, switched off the engine in the driveway and looked at his house. The blue slated roof was shiny with rain, the grey walls unpainted and the garden tiled for low maintenance. The windows were dark and white-framed, everything neat, orderly and sterile. He sat looking for a good while and decided he could not face entering, he restarted the car and returned instead to the gendarmerie. There Laura's message and the information on the two families were waiting.

Laura's message confirmed Espadrels as the focus of the investigation.

The Boussés had moved away to the Midi Pyrenees where they were tenant farmers. Their Espradels property was simply abandoned.

The Soula file, however, held some surprises. There was no uncle in Avignon, Hercules had simply fallen off the radar sometime around the time of Genevieve Boussé's disappearance.

*A*s the terror intensified: the bishop of Mende called for prayers to be said, all around the diocese, to give rise to another Saint George. While the people prayed the Beast caught and killed it's 60$^{th}$ victim, Delphine Courtiol from Saint-Méry, a mother, in broad daylight.

From all over the Kingdom, heroes offered their services to clear Gevaudan of its monster. Even lowly lark hunters dreamed of inflicting the decisive gunshot that would make a man 9400 pounds richer. Therefore another big hunt was organized: Captain Duhamel drew men from 73 parishes; 20 000 responding to his appeal.

The regional lords took charge of operations and this formidable army took the field on February 7th. With the countryside covered with a new fall of snow it was easy to track the Beast. Five peasants from Malzieu shot at it: it fell screaming but immediately got back on its feet and disappeared.

The next day, the Beast decapitated a fourteen-year old girl, so a trap was made of her remains, placed appropriately in a hollow and surrounded by marksmen. But the Beast, perhaps sensing danger, did not approach.

The discouragement was immense, these fruitless hunts, the demands of the Duhamel's Dragoons, and the expense incurred by their stay was bankrupting the department. Besides which farming, its economic mainstay was paralysed, without cattle at pasture and the markets deserted. Such a disaster had never before befallen the Gevaudan and no one could foresee the end of the plague.

September 7

As Gadret drifted in and out of drug-induced consciousness he dreamed vivid and troubling dreams.

He was deep in a dark forest of huge pines cowering under the rotting hulk of a fallen tree in a hollow surrounded by the bleached bones and skulls of people. He was hiding from something unseen in the trees, his fear a weight on his chest like a wound. Beyond the hollow a presence lurked, stalking, searching among the tangle of trees. It circled around, he could hear the crack of branches cracking underfoot as it came ever closer to his hiding-place. He was aware of heavy breathing, his own, and that of the approaching predator, its jaws and teeth clicking as it sniffed him out.

Gadret sought escape, strangely he was clothed in his finest dress uniform, all soiled with a rank mixture of mud and blood, his polished shoes heavy with clay. His pistol felt like a popgun, small and ineffective in his hand and there seemed no way out of his situation. He knew he must wait, curled in his sanctuary for the beast to come closer, for its muzzle to probe under one side of the tree-trunk while he escaped from the other.

At last the sniffing muzzle found the entry to his hiding-place, sniffing and snorting, its long pink tongue slobbering over enormous yellow fangs. Catching his scent it began scratching with its great claws at the gap beneath the tree.

Sensing his moment, Gadret rolled away from the probing snout, got to his feet and ran blindly into the trees. A great snarl behind him signalled that the Beast was aware of his flight and he sensed its great form arch over the tree in a tremendous bound.

Blinding lights suddenly illuminated the great grey-brown beast, which turned sharply under a volley of bullets from camouflaged legionnaires who erupted from the undergrowth. The Beast roared in distress, fell momentarily, then shook itself and ran headlong along a barely discernible track that ran through the trees.

An old Willys Jeep appeared with Laura Platigny at its wheel and she ordered him into the passenger seat. The ancient machine jolted and slid along, pursuing the elusive form that ran ahead. Perhaps the animal was wounded, it appeared that it was slowing, or they were gaining, as it headed for a cleft in the rocks of the mountainside.

Suddenly, inexplicably, the Jeep stopped. Laura was looking in panic at the lifeless controls as Gadret became aware of steam, smoke and oil issuing from bullet holes that had appeared in the Jeep's bonnet. The Beast disappeared around the shoulder of an enormous boulder astride which stood the old farmer Soula, red eyes blazing, coolly reloading his rifle...

* * *

The beeping made him stir. He opened his eyes to see blinking orange lights on a grey box by the bedside. His chest hurt as did his throat and the back of his left hand.

He slowly came to consciousness, becoming aware that he was lying in a raised bed, in a grey room with stainless steel fittings. A hospital room, he correctly deduced. He was alone with the machines. There were tubes and cables that snaked under his bedclothes. With great effort he pulled himself up in the bed and pulled back the sheets. He was naked, his torso a mass of bruising, all purples and yellows. The wires ran to pick-ups taped to his chest. The tubes to a catheter in his left hand and a colostomy receiver taped to his private parts. He detached these first, then he pulled the wires from his chest, grimacing as the movement tore off some of his pubic hairs. The machines went mad, alarms shrilly sounding in the room and somewhere in the corridor. A sound of fast footsteps and a nurse with a concerned face looked in at him from the doorway.

"Hello nurse," Gadret said, "Any chance of something to eat? I'm starving."

* * *

129

With the nurse's capable aid, in some pain, Gadret managed to sit upright and then swing his legs over the side of the bed. His legs almost buckled as he put his weight on them to stand. After some attempts, and with the nurse's continued support he managed some paces. Then he settled in the armchair to rest.

"Could you bring me my things?" he asked.

The nurse soon returned clutching a plastic bag with little in it, just his mobile phone his wallet and his warrant card. "Your clothes were too bloody and damaged to salvage." she explained as she collected the empty food tray from the bedside table.

Gadret nodded and picked up his mobile phone. He phoned an off-duty colleague and asked him to bring some clothes and personal effects from his quarters to the hospital. The attendant nurse looked horrified. "You are not ready to be discharged yet sergeant," she said, sternly.

Gadret ignored her and closed his eyes. When he re-opened them his colleague was grinning down at him, "I brought your things, they're over there on the bed. I hate to tell you this Gadret, but you look awful!"

Gadret felt too sore to disagree, he got up from the armchair. Again, his head span and he almost fainted with the unfamiliar pain caused by movement. His colleague caught him.

"I'll be alright," said Gadret, regaining composure, "Just give me a hand to change into my own clothes will you?"

Gadret was determined to leave the hospital, despite the opposition of the nurses and his colleague. He demanded pain-killing medication to go. He knew his pain was obvious but he no longer cared to loiter in the sterile limbo of the ward. Amid a clamour of disapproval he was reluctantly given the medicines he asked for and released into the care of his protesting friend. The nurses, peeved, but still in professional caring-mode, took him through the hospital to the car park in a wheelchair. With some difficulty, because the seatbelt ran across his injured chest, he sat in the passenger seat and directed his friend to take him to the gendarmerie.

* * *

"My God Gadret, you look like death warmed up!" exclaimed Maury as the Sergeant entered his office.

"I feel like death." Gadret conceded with a wry smile.

Maury had an old leather sofa against one wall of his office which looked as if it had recently served as a bed. Maury shifted some covers from it, "Here, sit down," he said.

"It's good to see you sergeant, I didn't think they'd discharge you quite so soon."

"I discharged myself," explained Gadret, wincing as he tried to get himself comfortable on the sofa. "I want to go back on the case...that bloody old farmer who shot me was hiding something..."

Maury simply nodded, "My thoughts too. In fact I was arranging to go to the Soula place with a gendarme and a four-wheel-drive vehicle."

"I'd like to come."

"Are you sure you're up to it?"

"I'll be fine, the more eyes you've got the better...but we'd better take rifles...What are the latest developments?"

Maury explained, "Sanchez reckons that Espradels is at the centre of a series of recent incidents. Sixteen years ago a young girl from that same village, a Genevieve Boussé, was reported to have been taken by the Beast. What we didn't know at the time was that she and Soula's son were sweet on one another. We were told he was away farming at his uncle's in Avignon, but there is no uncle and there's been no record of Hercules Soula since his girlfriend disappeared."

* * *

131

When they pulled up at the Soula's farmyard, old Estoup was there seeing to the livestock, but he scuttled off as soon as he saw the word 'Gendarmerie' and a tricolour shield emblazoned on the Jeep's drab olive side.

The gendarme detailed to drive and accompany the two detectives was Maury's old compatriot Lalande who quickly located the farmhouse key under a flowerpot on the veranda.

Once again, they looked carefully through the paraphernalia littering the house's shelves. While Maury and Lalande worked their way methodically through the living and sitting rooms, Gadret headed for the kitchen. It was he that called out first, Maury found him in the room-sized pantry pointing with a puzzled expression at a box full of baby's Formula milk. "What the heck does he want that for?"

Maury's mind whirred, Laura had said she's seen a baby on the treeline a mere stone's throw from the farm, this could surely not be coincidence...

* * *

Their search radiated outward from the farmhouse into the sheds and outbuildings through the paddocks and yards but there was nothing.

Gadret looked at Maury and said, with some reluctance, "We're going to have to follow the track up onto the mountain."

Maury sensed the sergeant's dread, it was difficult to revisit the site of so much trauma. "You could stay here, if you like Gadret, that ride's going to be rough on you."

Gadret though, was determined, "These modern jeeps have far softer suspension. I'll be alright if Lalande drives carefully. Besides I'd like to see where it all happened, it may jog a memory."

"Okay," said Maury, "It's your call. But we'll stop and come back another time if we have to."

Lalande had heard this conversation and he began preparing the jeep for the journey up the track by putting the rifles in special racks between the seats, so they could be reached quickly if needed. He also partially deflated the tyres to improve grip – a trick that old hands kept to themselves.

* * *

Eventually they reached the same area where the track petered out to almost nothing. Lalande halted the jeep and Gadret leaned forward to pull his ribcage away from the seat-back. Taking a rifle Lalande directed the others to remain in the car while he took a quick look around. He got back in a few minutes later. "This isn't the end of the track," he reported, "a vehicle looks to have traversed the slope to get to the Chaos over there." His finger pointed at the chaos, the term used to describe a discreet area of talus, a jumble of weirdly weathered stones on the mountainside about a kilometre away, standing above a smudge of silver birches - their leaves yellow against the dark of the rocks.

Lalande quietly awaited Maury's instructions, Maury turned to Gadret, "What do you think?"

Gadret was looking at the ferns beside the stationary vehicle, just able to make out the flattened and bruised plants he'd crushed while avoiding Soula's bullets. There was little more to see, no memory of any significance jogged by these bleak surroundings. "Let's give it a look." he said.

* * *

It was hard to know where to start, from afar the talus had seemed to cover quite a small area, up close the stone field was enormous, its rocks so massive, densely juxtaposed and packed together that it seemed impossible to negotiate. All three men gripped high powered rifles ensuring that their advance was covered as they moved methodically into the chaos. They gave up ten minutes later when they came to the foot of an insurmountable buttress.

133

Aiming to get to a high vantage point they began skirting the rocks at the base of the buttress when they were assailed by a noxious stench on the breeze. All three men gagged and covered their mouths and noses to prevent breathing the foul air. Something, somewhere was definitely dead and rotting amid this labyrinth. A dark smear stained another wall of rock, at its base was a midden. A murder of crows arose on jagged wings, cawing in annoyance as the approaching policemen disturbed their meal. The midden seemed full of putrefying offal and excrement. There were tangles of grey, white and purple intestines and other gruesome entrails in which swam other unspeakable objects.

The stench made the policemen reluctant to approach, so Maury directed the others to watch over him as he shouldered his rifle, covered his nose and mouth with a sleeve, and went forward for a closer look into the vile pool. There were bones, fleece fragments, hide, skin and other detritus floating amid the entrails and shit. A spherical object tangled in pale fronds caught the Inspector's eye and with horror Maury realised he was looking at Fabienne Sonnester's severed head, her pale eyes dull and sightless, her mouth grimacing in a frozen scream. Bile rose in the veteran detective's mouth and he vomited as he realised that floating beside the head were the girl's detached hands and feet.

Wiping his mouth free of the stinging acid taste of his own stomach contents Maury made his way back to his waiting companions. Gadret and Lalande looked at him questioningly when they caught sight of his ashen face. "We've found what's left of the German girl!" Maury explained, "We need to call for reinforcements..."

Maury's orders were cut short by an echoing wail. Surprised, the men looked up to see that it emanated from a naked and dirty child standing atop the bluff overlooking the midden. As they looked the child, clamped his filthy hands over his mouth, turned on his heel and disappeared into the mouth of a dark cleft in the rocks.

Maury made a quick decision, "Lalande, can you return to the jeep and radio for reinforcements? Gadret and I will attempt to find the child."

Lalande looked a little hesitant at first, then nodded and made off cautiously in the direction they had come.

"Are you up for this?" Maury asked, when he saw that Gadret was obviously still in pain and discomfort.

Gadret looked at the rocks that blocked their path and shook his head, "...I can get to the top of this big rock here and provide covering fire for both you and Lalande," he suggested.

Maury nodded, "Alright, cover both of us."

Gadret, with some difficulty reached the top of the rock, finding it commanded a good view of the lower slopes of the chaos. Lalande was picking his way towards the encircling birches, Maury was hauling himself over rocks trying to negotiate a path to take him to the dark cleft into which the child had disappeared.

Putting the telephoto sight to his eye, Gadret swept his sights over Lalande's back and along the route that would lead him back to the jeep. Were his eyes playing tricks?   A grey boulder appeared to have moved in the bracken between the gendarme and the vehicle. He retrained his sights on the rock – it was quite static and Gadret was about to switch his attention to the inspector when he realised that the stone's grey surface was being rippled by the breeze. He was not looking at stone, he was looking at fur! Lalande was heading straight into an ambush.

Breathing slowly out and letting his heartbeat slow Gadret trained the cross-hairs on the grey form, centred on its lowest visible part, flicked off the safety and squeezed the trigger. A sudden report echoed around the surrounding rocks as the high velocity round was loosed. Eyes still glued on his target Gadret saw the grey form jerk and fall back into the bracken.

When Gadret's shot rang out Maury stopped in his tracks, he looked back at the sergeant kneeling atop his sentinel rock, his rifle steadily trained in the other direction. Realising that his comrades may be in trouble and his first duty was to their safety Maury reluctantly began retracing his steps.

Lalande had frozen before the sharp report echoed through the rocks, it had been preceded by a whoosh that he recognised as the passage of the high velocity round over his head and the thump as the bullet found its mark. He remained rooted and alert as an absolute silence descended.

Keeping his eye to the rubber bellows of the sights, Gadret trained his rifle on the area of heather into which his prey had fallen, watching carefully for any sign of movement. Gradually he relaxed his finger's grip on the trigger and began sweeping his sights methodically and carefully ever outwards from the area where his bullet had impacted, still   watchful for signs of movement. He returned his sights regularly to the centre-point of heather and continued sweeping until he had sighted both Lalande and the drab outline of the jeep. Then he raised his arm and shouted "All clear," waiting for Lalande to acknowledge the signal with a slight nod.

Gadret then scrambled from his vantage point to join Maury who'd arrived at the base of the rock. Cautiously, systematically, they worked their way to Lalande who was stilled keyed and in a position of acute readiness. As they went Gadret explained the situation to Maury.

"Do you think you got it?" Asked Maury.

"I think so, but we need to make sure."

When they reached Lalande, all three advanced line abreast through the bracken. They came across obvious evidence that Gadret's bullet had indeed found its mark, in the heather and ferns was a trail of blood and marks where the creature appeared to have dragged itself away.

"Looks like you wounded it...we'd better be doubly careful now."

Remarked Lalande, indicating - with a turn of his head - that the tracks were leading back into the chaos.

Gadret said nothing, his mouth a grim tight line.

Maury looked into the higgledy-piggledy boulder field, sensing that from somewhere in the talus they were being watched. "Let's call for help."

Back at the jeep Lalande raised control at Mende, Gadret swallowed a fistful of painkillers and Maury retrieved binoculars from the glove-box. Just as he put them to his eyes Lalande caught his attention and handed him the radio's headset. Maury listened to the controller, then simply said, "I understand," as he switched off the receiver.

He turned to the others, "We can't get help for a while there's a stand-off with armed robbers taking place at a motorway service station. Apparently they have hostages and that's taking priority."

Gadret looked at his watch, "And it's lunchtime," he growled sarcastically.

"What shall we do?" asked Lalande.

More wailing rose from the talus, it was definitely human, definitely someone young or female, and unquestionably anguished and it answered the question for them. Setting their faces, making determined preparations they turned back to the chaos.

Almost inevitably, as they began to traverse the rocks the rain began to fall in large, ever persistent drops. This obliterated the already indistinct trail of blood droplets, that the wounded creature had left.

No-one spoke but they turned as one towards the area of the midden and the dark cave entrance above it. With the rain came a descending cloud base, conditions underfoot became treacherous on the wet slippery boulders. Methodically, the policemen sought handholds and footholds, pulled and pushed each other along until gasping they were atop the ledge upon which the child had recently stood. At least the rain was suppressing the revolting smell of the midden below them.

Maury suddenly cocked his head and shushed the others while listening intently over the roar of the rain. From the cavern's depths came the sound of sobbing.

For one awful moment Maury thought that they have to proceed into the dark cave entrance blindly, until the ever-efficient Lalande drew a torch from his webbing belt. They sloped their rifles against the rock and unholstered their service pistols in the narrow opening, grateful to at least find a little shelter from the now teeming rain.

"You okay to lead?" asked Maury as he touched Lalande lightly on his arm. The gendarme nodded, clipping his torch to his pistol.

Maury then looked at Gadret who was stooping, white-faced and obviously exhausted, "Are you okay?"

Gadret smiled weakly and nodded.

"I'll bring up the rear then," said Maury "Pass me your rifles."

Figuring that any encounter they might now have within the narrow confines would be at close quarters the rifles were temporarily redundant. With dexterous movements Maury removed their magazines and made the rifles safe before standing them carefully in a dry corner, then he nodded, "Let's go."

The cave's interior was a rancid gloom that Lalande's flash-light revealed to be   a narrow passage formed under the tipped stones of the chaos, its walls either sour black peat or matt grey stone, the floor uneven well-worn mud. It was difficult for Gadret and Maury to stumble sightlessly behind Lalande and when he halted about twenty-five metres into the passage they were glad. They pricked their ears to find that the sobbing had stopped and except for their own heavy breathing the channel was as quiet as the grave.

Maury tried to look past Gadret and Lalande at what was being lit by the flash-light. The passage appeared to turn sharply around a boulder.

A whispered, "Okay." from Maury sent them cautiously forward. But once they'd rounded the boulder Lalande came to another sudden stop, Maury and Gadret sensing him tense craned their necks to peer past him.

The cavern opened into a high chamber into which weak natural light leaked from gaps between the rocks. There appeared to be ragged plastic and cloth sheeting hanging on the walls. The floor was littered with various junk - old car seats, tyres and other vaguely discerned objects.

But what grabbed the attention was the pale flesh of the boy-child, luminescent against the dark figures who stood either side of him. The figures looked to be Neanderthal, as Lalande's beam swept over them. One was obviously an adult male, heavily-bearded, his hair a tangled mess and he wore a medley of clothing and furs. The other, a woman, was similarly dressed but her hair was long and well-cared for. Both stared venomously at the beam of the torch.

Behind the figures, laying on the ground unmoving was a large grey-brown furred creature with a three-clawed paw clearly visible.

While his colleagues trained their weapons on the strange group Maury stepped forward, extending a reassuring hand to the child. In obvious fear the boy pulled away from the advancing detective, and clung to the female's legs, whimpering.

Maury once more attempted to be reassuring, "You're safe now, we're policemen..."

The woman hissed and shielded the child, the man tensed himself as if ready to attack.

For everyone's benefit Maury held up his hands and explained what he was about to do, "I am inspector Maury from Mende, the men behind me are also policemen. I am going to put my gun away," he said, holstering his pistol with his right hand and keeping his left raised. "Please step aside so I can see what's behind you."

The man and woman closed ranks, standing shoulder to shoulder looking determined to stand their ground.

"At least let the child come forward."

Again, the couple were non-compliant. It looked as if the impasse would continue had the beast behind the couple and child not started slowly rising. The loud reports of pistols barking made ears ring as Gadret and Lalande's hand-guns shot flame and lead into the reviving creature.

An acrid spiral of gun-smoke rose in the half-light and the ensuing second of silence, seemed interminable as Maury looked at a terrible and tragic tableau. The woman, clutching the pale-fleshed child to her breast, had fallen to her knees, silently wailing, with her free arm extended imploringly toward the grey-brown furred beast. The man had also fallen to his knees, his head slumped forward on his chest, his arms hanging forlornly at his sides. Beyond them an arm and hand clutching a three-pronged hoe fell from the folds of pelt.

For a stunned moment Maury's head reeled, his ears ringing from the noise of the pistols firing in such a confined space. But he knew too that everyone, except the policemen would be paralysed in shock. Now was the time for action.

He stepped forward to the man, "Hercules?" he asked softly. The man looked up and nodded in obvious surprise. Maury beckoned to Gadret, "Cuff him. Be gentle." he now turned to the woman, "Genevieve?" The woman nodded sadly, still clutching the child. "Is this your child?" again the woman nodded. This time Maury looked to Lalande who was already stepping forward with his handcuffs.

Now it was time to take a closer look at the "Beast". Dressed almost like a native American shaman, with a wolf-skin mantle, its head a macabre mask, lay an adolescent giant, his hair a dark tangle of curls. The mouth was open in death's painful grimace revealing a mouthful of teeth filed to sharp points. Blood oozed dark and slow from bullet-holes in the well-muscled torso, staining the hide and deerskin

140

pyjamas he wore. But for an enormous hump that grotesquely distorted his shoulders and upper back giving him a massively top-heavy appearance, the young man would have been an Adonis.

With Hercules and Genevieve handcuffed, the three policemen started looking carefully around the cave.

The larder was a gruesome sight, behind the hanging covers, strips of meat of were hung to dry, some undoubtedly human. There were tins of food, utensils, a water pail and a gas camping stove in one corner. There was one paillasse on the floor, on which the body of the 'beast' lay, generous enough to accommodate a family.

While exploring a dark corner Lalande called out, "I can feel fresh air here, I think there may be another entrance." With that he squeezed himself into the fissure and disappeared from view. A few seconds later he reappeared nodding, "This seems to be the main way in, it leads to the top of the chaos."

Gadret was looking at a pile of clothing, he picked up and held aloft a blood-spattered item for them to see. It was a torn and bloody, grey fleece hoodie with 'Technische Universität Dortmund' emblazoned American-style across its front.

Maury's flesh was crawling, the iron stench of blood and death was overpowering, it was time to get some fresh air. "Lend me the torch Lalande, I'll go back for the rifles."

Gadret tasted rising bile in the back of his mouth; the grim mementoes of death hanging there, the pile of clothing pillaged from the dead, the cave a small factory of death - it somehow reminded him of German Death Camps – the pathetic detritus of human beings butchered.

His side was aching and fatigue weighed his limbs as he continued his forensic search of the cavern. He looked over at the handcuffed couple and child, the boy looked back at him with wide-eyed wonder then hid his head back in his mother's breast.

Suddenly, breathlessly, Maury returned from the midden passage,

"The rifles have gone!" he reported.

The three policemen conferred and agreed that they needed to leave the lair and return with their prisoners to the jeep.

Maury was sure that someone was out there in the rain, probably lying in wait, but it was better to take their chances than wait for darkness to fall, their torch to fail, and be vulnerable to attack in unfamiliar surroundings.

Maury ordered Hercules and Genevieve to their feet and they sullenly complied, the boy still clinging to his mother. Gadret found some vaguely suitable clothing in a pile and helped Genevieve to dress him. Lalande then led the way cautiously back to the jeep in the cleansing relief that was the rain.

Their exit brought them out at the top edge of the talus, they could skirt it rather than traverse it to get to the jeep. Maury hoped that whoever had removed the rifles had not interfered with their one mode of transport, or was drawing a bead on them as they accompanied their prisoners down to it.

They reached the car without drama and it appeared unmolested. After securing the family into the rear seats with Gadret covering them from the front passenger seat, Lalande used the radio to raise the Controller in Mende and outline their situation, he listened carefully to the reply and then turned to Maury, "A section will meet us at the Soula place with some paramedics. They are sending up a forensics team as soon as they can, who will have to be brought up here."

"Alright," said Maury, "Are you okay to escort them?" Lalande nodded.

Maury looked across at Gadret, "I think the sergeant needs to get some rest. I'll take these three back to the gendarmerie for interview. Did you tell them we need a social worker for the child?" Again, Lalande nodded.

"Okay, let's get back to the farm," ordered Maury as he rounded the jeep to sit in the rear jockey seat.

Everyone, except Lalande suffered in the drive back down the mountain; Gadret, due to his wounds and the fact that he was twisted in his seat to maintain an eye on the prisoners, Maury from being bounced mercilessly in the only seat outside the car's wheelbase, Hercules and Genevieve unable to stabilise themselves against the jerkier movements because of their handcuffs, the boy green-gilled and vomiting with travel sickness. The smell of sick sloshing in the footwell, above the already rancid smell of the unwashed family only added to their misery and made the thirty minute descent seem endless.

Back at the farm, a heavily armed detachment of gendarmes with four-by-fours and camouflaged fatigues were awaiting their arrival, as was a team of sapeur-pompier paramedics and their two ambulances.

When they alighted, eager hands helped Gadret and he was quickly accompanied to one ambulance by a team of paramedics, his wounds seeping blood through his t-shirt and jacket. The other paramedic team examined the family, a harassed-looking middle-aged woman briefly introduced herself as the Family Services Social Worker and oversaw their handling.

Maury meanwhile gathered the awaiting gendarmes and briefed them, "At the end of this track there is a large chaos. Within the rocks is a lair, a cave. In it you will find the body of our main suspect for the murder of the German students. The place is also littered with human and animal remains, collect and bag all you can. Lalande here will lead you to the site. He will also show you a second site where you will find Fabienne Sonnester's remains. Prepare yourselves, the place is a butcher's shop!

"Go carefully, we have reason to suspect that there may someone else hiding in the area, someone who made off with three police issue rifles..."

The gathered policemen looked at each other in wide-eyed alarm and began murmuring.

"However," Maury interrupted, pulling three magazines from his jacket pocket, "Without ammunition the rifles are next to useless. But whoever is up there may well be armed so, as I say, be very, very careful.

"I need a couple of you to help escort our prisoners back to the gendarmerie in Mende,"

A lieutenant detailed two cadets to accomplish this task and they attached themselves to the paramedic team. He then ordered his men to mount their vehicles and await Lalande's lead. But Lalande was circling his jeep looking puzzled, "Looks like we lost a Jerry can of fuel on the way down the mountain," he reported. The driver of another vehicle stepped forward with his spare can, Lalande thanked him and together they refuelled Lalande's jeep.

As the Gendarme's convoy started and warmed-up their engines another police vehicle, a forensics truck, roared into the yard and joined itself to the column. Headlamps were illuminated as another band of heavy rain shortened the evening and with a snarl the vehicles began snaking their way out onto the mountain.

\* \* \*

The ambulances took Maury, Gadret, Hercules, Genevieve, the child, the Social Worker and their gendarme escort back to the gendarmerie.

Despite continuing pain from his injuries, Gadret was determined to see the case to its conclusion, he was patched-up, given pain-relief and warned not to 'overdo' things.

\* \* \*

An ominous orange glow over the chaos met Lalande's convoy. Now he knew where the spare fuel had gone, it was the accelerant that had turned the cavern and its contents into an inferno.

There was little to do other than lead the forensics team to the midden, escorted by heavily-armed Gendarmes who aided their difficult passage over the tumult of rocks with heavy equipment.

* * *

Maury was not a happy man, the message from the chaos was bad news – the body of their main suspect and the bulk of their evidence was being consumed by flames, just as he was discovering that elective mutes cannot be communicated with by normal means. The only sound Hercules would make was a low growl when asked to change into overalls so his clothes could be examined. Likewise, Genevieve, although compliant, would shriek whenever she thought that she'd be separated from her child. The child, now calmer and eager to take the ham sandwiches he was offered seemed to also lack voice.

Maury needed specialist help, but he knew where to get it.

* * *

The midden slowly gave up its gruesome secrets; Fabienne's severed head, feet and hands, three police-issue rifles, various body parts, entrails, bones, hair and fur - all carefully bagged, labelled and returned to the forensics truck by a chain of policemen.

Lalande and three other gendarmes stood guard over this sinister scene, sweeping the sights of their rifles over the darkening perimeter. The flames from the burning cave were finally abating and plumes of smoke now wreathed the top of the mountain. One of his accompanying sentinels opened a crate and passed him something cylindrical and heavy, it was a night-sight which allow him to see heat-sources in the dark.

* * *

She was warmly curled up with her cat, a book and a cognac when her telephone rang. Belle was pleasantly surprised to hear Maury's voice, "Hello Belle, I haven't called at a bad time have I?"

"No, no, not at all," replied Belle, wondering where this conversation might lead.

145

"I need your help."

Her heart fluttered a little, those words, from Maury, were a surprise. "Of course..."

"We have Hercules Soula and Genevieve Boussé in custody. I need your help to interview them."

Her heart lurched in surprise, then sank a little in disappointment, but she was honoured by the challenge.

"Give me ten minutes," she said.

* * *

"There's something in the treeline one hundred metres east," reported one of the guards.

Lalande turned his sights to look, a pale form in the green luminescence of the sights confirmed his companion's words. "I see it," he affirmed. He refocused the sight to sharpen the image, "It looks like there's a person hiding up there."

As senior officer Lalande took charge, "Keep your sights on the target," he said. Then he motioned to Julien, a capable man he knew quite well, "Julien, you come with me. We'll outflank the target and try to capture him."

Together, Lalande and Julien picked their way through the rocks of the chaos until they reached the cover of ferns at its base. "I'll go right, you go left," Lalande directed. Stealthily Julien disappeared into the darkness. Lalande too began picking his way along a long arc that would terminate in the trees a little way behind the person hiding in the woods.

* * *

On arrival at the gendarmerie, Belle was met by Maury at the front desk and led into its heart. She was pleased to see that his eyes softened upon seeing her, though his body language made it clear that he was highly stressed.

146

As they went Maury outlined the situation and Belle was confident that she would be able help communicate with the two elective mutes. When he asked who she thought should be interviewed first, Belle was decisive, "Genevieve," she said.

* * *

Slowly Lalande inched nearer his prey, unseen, somewhere ahead under the trees. He trusted that Julien would be in a similar position somewhere to his right.

Using utmost stealth, controlling his breathing and heart-rate, pacing each step carefully he advanced until he could see a dark figure silhouetted against the afterglow emanating from the chaos.

A sharp crack startled him, at first he thought it was a gunshot, it came from where he supposed Julien to be. The noise also startled their quarry who rose up and began running headlong down the mountain. The dark figure was clutching something in the crook of one arm and waving a long-barrelled gun in the other, leaping awkwardly through the bracken.

Lalande swore and charged after the fleeing man, he heard Julien's voice shout a warning then for the second time that day he heard a bullet zip past and the bang of a gunshot. The fugitive faltered, then fell, his own gun spitting flame uselessly into the air as his finger tightened involuntarily on the trigger.

Lalande continued charging forward until he hurled himself onto the dark form outstretched in the bracken. He chopped down on the hand that was desperately trying to reach the dropped shotgun, aware of a smell of body odour and fuel as he ordered the squirming man to stay still. The man complied and craned his neck to look at the policeman just as Julien's torch lit the scene. To Lalande's complete surprise he found that they had captured old Estoup.

Julien was gasping for breath, "I stepped on a rotten branch," he explained.

147

Lalande simply nodded in understanding.

* * *

Maury was impressed, Belle had quickly gained Genevieve's confidence by introducing herself as a teacher from her old school and talking about the teachers and times that Genevieve knew. She signed as she spoke and gradually Genevieve signed her responses back.

Soon Genevieve agreed to answer Maury's questions, she sat with her child on one side of the table that dominated the room while Belle sat with Maury on the other. Belle's close proximity, her confidence and the smell of her perfume were an intoxicating cocktail and Maury found himself enjoying a small 'frisson' of pleasure. But now the formal interview could begin, he raised a hand, and behind the one-way mirror Gadret monitoring from the observation cell began recording.

* * *

Gadret looked in astonishment at the note from Lalande's team, passed to him by an apologetic administrator.

The team had shot and wounded an armed man near the chaos. This had turned out to be the old farmer from Espradels, Estoup, who smelled strongly of fuel and was found to be carrying a wolf-pelt. His injuries were not life-threatening and he was presently being sent for medical attention to the hospital in Mende.

The interview with Genevieve seemed to be ending, Gadret would pass this nugget on to Maury, maybe the Inspector could figure out what the hell was going on?

* * *

The arrival of sapeur-pompiers in a trio of scarlet four-wheel-drive fire trucks, meant that the forensics team would shortly be able to enter the cavern. The specialist gendarmes oversaw the firemen, ensuring that no remaining evidence was further damaged or destroyed. Gratefully, in this interlude, the other gendarmes rotated their duties

148

and snatched rations, knowing this was liable to be a long night. Lalande rued his decision to remain rather than escort Estoup to Mende, at least there he'd get some rest, today had been a very long and eventful day.

* * *

"Are you okay to continue?" Maury asked in concern.

Belle's countenance had changed during the interview, she was looking drawn and haunted.

"I never imagined that such things were happening, right here on our doorstep..." she replied.

"A coffee perhaps?" asked Maury.

Belle nodded assent and Maury asked an aide to see to her and show her to the rest-room, "I need to see to some other things. Give me ten minutes and then we'll try talking to Hercules."

While Belle was escorted away, Maury stepped into the observation cell. "Did you get all that?" he asked Gadret.

"Yes," said the sergeant, "But you need to see this." he added, passing Lalande's note.

"Estoup?" Maury exclaimed incredulously, "What the hell is going on up there?"

Gadret looked blank and shrugged.

"Okay, okay..." murmured Maury lapsing into pensive silence. He passed the note back, "You want to go to talk with Estoup? Find out if he really is part of all this?"

Gadret looked reluctant but he agreed. "I'll go, maybe I can get a pretty nurse to re-dress my wounds," he joked.

* * *

Hercules refused outright to talk, he would not give either Belle or

Maury eye contact, he sat opposite them rocking in his seat, staring at fixed point in space, somewhere on the floor behind them.

* * *

The lieutenant called for Lalande. "You've been in there before," he said, indicating the cave, "Put this on and see if you can make some sense of what we're looking at."

He passed Lalande white paper overalls and a fully enclosed respirator with attached headlamps and movie camera. Once the suit was donned, a similarly clad forensics man stepped forward with some flags on stiff spikes. "I want you to enter the cave very carefully," he said, "As you go, see what you can remember being in there. Put a flag on anything you can positively identify. The flags are numbered. Once you've placed a flag you need to tell me the number and what it is you think you have found. I'll be right behind you keeping a record. Is that clear?"

Lalande nodded, the forensics officer reached out and switched on the super-bright headlamps on his helmet, gave a thumbs-up and motioned to the rocks, "Okay then, let's go!"

* * *

Maury walked Belle out to her car, sensing that she was having difficulty coming to terms with Genevieve's revelations, he tried to be reassuring, "Things like this do happen, but rarely..."

She stopped and looked him directly in the eyes, "And you deal with this routinely?"

"No. Just as they arise."

She lifted a hand tenderly to his stubbly cheek, her eyes welling with tears, "You poor thing," she whispered, slipping into the driver's seat.

He stood in the dark and watched her drive away as, inevitably, his mobile phone rang.

"Allo?"

"It's Gadret. I'm on my way back. Estoup is in surgery and we won't be able to interview him for several hours."

"Then go home and get some rest."

"But..."

"That's an order Sergeant."

"Yes, Sir."

* * *

He felt like an astronaut in the suit, the helmet amplified the sound of his own breathing and the curve of the visor distorted the peripheral image at the edge of his field of vision.

The interior of the cave was black with charred remnants still steaming from the damping of the firemen's hoses.

Methodically Lalande identified everything he recognised until he reached the remains of the paillasse. Strangely it appeared that the fire had not burned as intensely at this end of the cave, the form of the hunchback was plain to see, the wolf skull fused by melted flesh to the hunchback's. The sharpened teeth were a frightening white grimace in the red-flesh remains of the broad-boned face. The body had obviously been moved post-mortem, last time he'd seen it, it had been curled into a foetal ball the face down, now it was on its back arms crossed over the chest, as if laid out for a Wake. Under it the pelts and hides, grey and brown were singed but mostly intact, the paillasse almost undamaged.

* * *

Inside the observation cell Maury was reviewing footage of Genevieve's interview, he noticed a repeated gesture made when there was a pause in proceedings, she would hold out both arms, her palms downward, make a patting gesture and then cradle herself.

His phone vibrated; a message from Lalande, "Body of hunchback moved post-mortem by person unknown, perhaps Estoup? See attached video file." It was the grim footage from Lalande's helmet camera.

Maury replied, "Need tattoo number from wolf pelt."

Another vibration, a missed call from a private number, he rang back. A familiar clipped male voice answered immediately, the police commissioner, "Ah Maury, I hear there's been a breakthrough in the Sonnester case."

"Yes Sir, a few loose ends to tie up..." Maury began explaining, but his commander cut him off, "You have the perpetrator though?"

"I think so." replied Maury cautiously.

"Yes or no?" the commissioner pressed him.

"Most likely," Maury conceded.

"Right. I'm calling a press conference for the morning, I'd like you to outline your investigations. Keep it upbeat, we need the Press to see us in a positive light after today's earlier debacle..." the commissioner explained that the stand-off in the petrol station had resulted in the armed robbers spiriting themselves away with 17,000 Euros right under the noses of the cream of Mende's security forces.

"I'll do my best sir."

"Right, Hotel de France at 10am sharp. Invite your investigation team along, they've got multimedia facilities at the hotel, it would be good to have you do something other than talk...Oh, and one more thing..."

"Yes sir?"

"Try to make an impression will you? It reflects on all of us..." the commissioner's parting barb was softened by a chuckle as he replaced the receiver.

*I*n Normandy, a certain old gentleman called d'Enneval had nightmares about the Beast. Being a wolf hunter of great repute, he went to Versailles and succeeded in securing an audience with the King. He had killed, he said an estimated 1200 wolves. He swore to his Majesty that not only would he kill the Beast but he would return with the stuffed animal so the court could witness his success. The King agreed to commission him, wished him good luck, and d'Enneval took the road south.

He arrived in Saint-Flour with his son, two steppers and six enormous mastiffs twenty days later. To spare their dogs, the Normans had covered the distance slowly and the Beast took advantage of this to devour around 20 children.

d'Enneval prepared himself methodically: he wanted to study the unusual game he was about to hunt. He explored the country to see how the land lay; he found tracks and noticed that the Beast could leap over 28 feet in one bound. He concluded that "This Beast is not easy to catch". Moreover, he did not want any rivalry and declared that he would not attempt anything if Duhamel and his dragoons were still in the field.

While discussions and little intrigues were taking place among the local governors the Beast did not fast, in Ally it devoured a 40 year-old woman, in the village of Fayet it ate a 20 year-old girl; it entered a Mallevieillette warehouse and mauled a 5 year-old girl. Similar successive atrocities occurred in places so distant to another that one could not explain how it covered ground so fast. This constant ranging inspired such a terror in France that similar incidents were reported in Soissons, it seemed the Beast was devastating both Auvergne and Picardy at the same time!

d'Enneval reiterated that he wanted to hunt without contest, but

*Duhamel stubbornly refused to leave...and all the while the Beast was eating people!*

*As expected, the King's Norman champion prevailed: Duhamel beat a retreat with his soldiers and left the country. No-one doubted that now, the wolf hunter would triumph over the Beast. However, after three months of hunting with an army of some 10,000 peasants he only managed to kill a poor female wolf, weighing in at barely 40 pounds, her belly containing only hare fur.*

*Desperate, d'Enneval resorted to methods unworthy of his great reputation; he poisoned a cadaver and used it to bait a trap near a wood where the monster had been reported. The Beast simply ripped the cadaver free of the trap, made off with it and dined well.*

*After 10 weeks of beats and ambushes, shooting and traps, it seemed the Beast was laughing at the people, their bullets and their poison. Even the most enthusiastic hunters became discouraged, d'Enneval complained that he was badly assisted, the peasants laughed at him and joked that he was unable to kill anything other than rabbits!*

September 8

The wound from the bullet hurt, but it hadn't done the damage the doctors had feared, he'd be on his feet in the morning.

Good, he had cattle to feed and a small kingdom to oversee. "Every cloud has a silver lining", the Soula affair was a Shakespearean tragedy in which he'd played a small part, but now he'd reap the reward of patience, "Good things come to he who waits", what would he do with the hectares of land that must surely now come his way, now that Soula had passed on? Hercules would surely not inherit? No, not his poor retarded nephew, a dumb wild-man who was more at home in the forest. No, the only relative to whom it could possibly now come was he, the brother of Soula's long dead wife, "Bless her soul", he – Estoup.

The old man chuckled to himself, "The police will come, but I will plead ignorance..." But then a dark thought crossed his mind. Who had left the wolf-pelt and the fuel can at the edge of the chaos? "The police will think it is me, poor Estoup!" And what eyes were upon him, drilling his back in the woods before the policeman cracked the twig underfoot that made him flee? But surely the Beast is dead?

* * *

Estoup's dogs came alive when they saw him step from the taxi. They bound over, their tails wagging their bodies in excitement at being reunited with their master. As the car drove off Estoup dropped to his haunches and reciprocated his dog's greeting allowing their pink tongues to tickle his ears as he stroked and slapped their hard short-furred flanks.

Presently, he led the dogs into the farmhouse kitchen where he donned blue overalls, rubber boots and changed his best flat-cap for his greasy work one. He opened a tin of food and spooned its contents into the dog's bowls, opened the windows while the dogs ate and then reached for the twelve-bore shotgun over the mantelpiece. He loaded a cartridge into each chamber and put spares into his pockets.

155

The dogs had soon finished and they gambolled in the doorway, eager to lead Estoup into the farmyard to complete his chores.

* * *

"Thank you all for coming," the commissioner was upbeat and smiling as he looked around at the gathered Press, senior police officers and the invited VIPs gathered in the conference room, "I invited you all here for an update. There has been a major breakthrough in one of our on-going cases, the case involving the German student Fabienne Sonnester. Without further ado let me turn proceedings over to our lead detective Inspector Maury."

Maury rose to his feet, extremely smart, clean-shaven and dressed in an expensive and becoming Italian suit. He felt stiff and uncomfortable, but he knew his wife had chosen well. He'd found the suit and a case full of laundered and ironed clothes awaiting him once he'd returned to his office from the holding cells in the small hours of the morning. He stood in front of a large interactive screen and looked at the sea of expectant faces; national, regional and local reporters with cameras, sound-recorders and notepads; senior policemen from Mende, le Puy and even an old colleague, Pierre, now Inspector General from Montpellier; and he was pleased to see that Gadret sat with Laura and Professor Sanchez in a back row.

He pressed the trigger which advanced the slide-show and two old photographs were displayed side-by-side on the screen, one a brooding little boy, the other an open-faced and radiant little girl. "These children are Hercules Soula and Genevieve Boussé, both from the hamlet of Espradels in the commune of Luc. They were both born in the village, just four months apart. Both came from local farming families, both had special educational needs and both went to a Special School here in Mende. As children they travelled together to the school, attended the same classes, played together in the playground and looked out for one another. Almost inevitably as they grew together, so they came to love one another..."

Maury paused, pressed the trigger and the slide now changed to project a picture of Genevieve as a pretty sad-eyed teen.

"Worried about the blossoming romance between their daughter and the son of a neighbour, that they seem to have for some reason despised, the Boussé family decided, when she was fourteen, to send Genevieve away to another Special School near Alés. As a result her behaviour deteriorated, although still doing well at school, she was withdrawn and refused to socialise with the other children. The head teacher wrote to alert her parents.

"Thinking that all their daughter needed was time and distance away from Hercules to get over him, they insisted that she remain at Alés even during holiday periods and forbade her from seeing him in the one long break during the summer when the school was closed. Consequently these two months became a living hell for the family, with Genevieve throwing tantrums and trying to escape to see her boyfriend. Indeed, her parents finally resorted to locking her in her room as punishment for her outbursts..."

A thumb-press triggered another slide transition, the screen now displayed a cropped picture of a stiff looking Hercules in his mourning suit, his haunted gaze looking at a point somewhere beyond the photographer.

"Mourning the loss of his one and only friend Hercules also underwent profound behavioural changes, he slowly withdrew from any interaction with others, first by refusing to attend school, then to run off into the wilds to hunt rather than help his parents out on the farm."

The photograph of Hercules expanded to reveal the full picture, his father Soula beside him hollow-eyed and identically clad.

"This is a picture of Hercules and his father at Madame Soula's funeral. A couple of hours after this photograph was taken Soula found his son trying to hang himself from a beam in the barn. Not only had the poor man to cope with losing his wife to cancer, to work his farm alone, but

157

he also had to care for an increasingly miserable and suicidal son.

"Somehow, we think he hatched a plan to ensure Hercules had something to live for, but first he had to make the boy disappear. So Soula encouraged his son in his love of the outdoors, to find shelter and to forage and hunt for food, but most of all to remain invisible and to avoid people. He told his neighbours and the authorities that Hercules had been sent to learn agriculture with an uncle near Avignon. No-one had any reason to doubt this was true, after all Provence is a much more amenable place to farm than Lozère.

"Sometime later Soula travelled to Alés, there he visited Genevieve at her school. The girl obviously knew him, a friendly neighbour passing through on his way to see his son in Avignon, so the staff there had no concerns. During this visit we believe that Soula asked Genevieve if she wanted to be with Hercules, and when she said yes he put his plan to her.

"When she returned to the family farm for the summer break she was to behave herself for the first few days, then she should escape to join Hercules who would be waiting for her in the woods. The plan was duly executed and the young couple ran off to make a new life for themselves. We suspect that there are some villagers who knew what was going on, but they had seen the girl mistreated, and they shrugged their shoulders and remained silent when they were interviewed by the investigators, or they fabricated another chapter in the life of Gevaudan's infamous Beast."

Maury advanced the slide to show newsreel footage of the gendarmerie teams searching ponds and making door-to-door enquiries at the time of Genevieve's disappearance.

"With the investigation meeting either this wall of silence or a free-flow of superstitious fantasy and unable to link Genevieve to Hercules or any evidence of foul play, it was presumed that the girl had simply run away from parents who had proven to be abusive. Her case remained an unsolved Missing Persons enquiry."

A trigger-press brought up a picture of the stunningly pretty Fabienne Sonnester, happily smiling at the photographer.

"What does all this have to do with the disappearance of this young woman? Well, Hercules and Genevieve managed to get by for over seventeen years by living off the land, hunting, stealing and poaching. They established camps all over the region, in caverns and dug-outs in the woods. To avoid discovery they rotated between these places..."

Sanchez' map with its mosaic of pins was projected.

"They did so well that they even managed to raise a small family. Their firstborn, a sturdy young son they named Thomas, was born within a year of their elopement – he would now be roughly sixteen years old – became a strong and adept hunter who took over from his father as the family's main provider. I'll return to Thomas in due course...

"Genevieve gave birth to several children in the most horrendously primitive conditions, but unfortunately most subsequently died when stricken by childhood illness, and some later on by malnutrition.

"In fact the family may have sustained this lifestyle had it not been for the effects of a catastrophic event that took place in Marvejols last year. There, a section of fence was crushed in a storm allowing a number of wolves to escape from the Wolf Park."

A click brought up a stunning portrait of grey wolves in snow, Maury stole a quick glance at Laura who was wide-eyed in astonishment before continuing.

"The family suddenly had to cope with the competition of another apex predator on their hunting grounds. The wolf pack started to deprive the family of its staple food source, the small game they caught in the mountains and forests. Despite Thomas trapping and killing two wolves, the damage had been done, the younger children and his parents were critically weakened by the effects of starvation.

"Desperate times call for desperate measures and Thomas, the family's hunter-gatherer, happened upon a freely available and reliable food source...human beings!"

The room, already hushed, fell into a deeper silence. At a button-press the screen went blank. No need for any gimmickry now thought Maury, the mention of cannibalism had everyone's complete horrified attention.

"We do not know for sure how many people fell victim to Thomas' hunting sprees – we have evidence to suggest at least four victims. Unfortunately, despite the availability of a new meat, two children died leaving just one of Thomas' siblings - a three-year old brother alive. This infant remained critically ill, so the family returned to Espradels to seek aid from old man Soula. He used veterinary medicines and supplements to nurse the family, but knew they had to return to the forest or risk discovery. He must also have have become aware of what they were doing to survive and having no solution, we believe that it was he who devised the wolf and animal skin costume that Thomas began to wear on his sorties. After all the resurrection of the 'Beast' had already masked their activities..."

Another trigger-press and the blank screen slowly displayed a grainy sepia photograph of a Native American shaman wearing a similar wolf-skin regalia.

"So now Thomas could hunt and kill as the Beast. It so happened that Fabienne Sonnester, camping in the isolated wilds, and her boyfriend Fausto Claudi crossed his path and paid the ultimate price..."

Maury held up a wickedly curved three-clawed hoe for the audience to see, "They were attacked with something like this. Fabienne was killed, Fausto fought for his life but fell to his death while being pursued. Fabienne's body was carried back to the family's lair to be butchered and eaten.

"There are other victims, one we are able to confirm as Alain Descartes, a civil servant, who chose to be fishing in the wrong spot at the wrong time. We found his forearm some eighty kilometres from where he disappeared, apparently Thomas liked to take along a snack as he was hunting..."

Again the drained faces turned and looked at one another in outright horror.

"Circumstances brought the investigation to Espradels, which Professor Sanchez..." Maury indicated the elderly academic, "had already identified as the hub of Thomas' attacks. There, on Soula's land we came upon the family's lair and evidence of their atrocities. During this operation, our main suspect, Thomas was shot and killed. Genevieve, Hercules and their youngest son were apprehended and are presently in safe custody here in Mende."

There Maury concluded. There was a short pause before the journalists began to murmur and the commissioner stepped into the Inspector's place to chair the rest of the briefing.

* * *

The old mule was the last animal he had to feed, it nuzzled its dusty grey muzzle into the feed-bag he hung on its stable door and crunched the oats noisily with its yellow teeth. The dogs lay waiting, looking at Estoup expectantly, as he picked up his old gun and carried it in the crook of his arm. Now he would see to the chores in the other part of his small kingdom – Soula's farm.

* * *

"I'm glad it wasn't your wolves," admitted Maury to Laura, as he caught up with her in the hotel car park, "Have you time for a coffee, or do you have to be somewhere?"

Laura smiled a puzzled smile, "No...I'd be delighted."

He put out the crook of his arm for her to take and escorted her back into the hotel, catching a glimpse of their reflection in a mirror as they passed, Maury was shocked to see that they made a handsome couple, he dashing in his tailored suit, she tall and elegant in her classic black dress.

161

He found a quiet table and they sat. Maury leaned forward and spoke quietly, "I wanted to explain what we think happened to you in Espradels."

Laura's body tensed, her eyes searched his face and she nodded almost imperceptibly.

"The young child you saw was recovering from illness and severe malnutrition. The family had returned to their lair at the top of Soula's mountain to get his help for the boy. Soula used antibiotics and animal supplements to treat the child , his grandson, but seemed to have worried that his diet was lacking calcium. So he was providing the family with milk formula. Genevieve, the boy's mother, told us that the child wandered off on the morning you were running in the area. Apparently, he wanted milk from his grandfather but took the wrong path. Thomas was sent to find him, and that is when your encounter took place."

Laura's eyes now searched Maury's, as if demanding truth, "Would he have killed and eaten me had he caught me?"

Maury returned her intense look and sighed, "Probably..."

* * *

The dogs eagerly accompanied their master through the village, sniffing at familiar and unfamiliar scents, cocking their legs against walls, tyres and shrubs as they passed. But they stopped dead at the entrance and looked at their master nervously as he stepped from the tarmac of the departmental road onto the ruts of the unmade lane. He went on a few paces but the dogs simply stood where they were, ears and eyes drooping apologetically, but they could not be coaxed any further even by soft words of encouragement or growls of command. Estoup's own hackles raised in annoyance, but also in fear – what could the dogs sense that he could not? Still, he was committed, there were animals that needed food and water at the other end of the track and he had the shotgun, with spare shells, for protection. Stupid dogs, let them run home!

Gadret was leaning against his car, enjoying the unfamiliar sunshine, as he waited for Maury in the car park of the gendarmerie. Soon the inspector arrived, greeted him and led the way towards his office.

As they passed the Custodial Suite, Maury paused to look in at their prisoners. In his cell, Hercules was standing, like a naughty schoolboy, in a far corner with his face to the wall. "I doubt we'll ever get anything out of him," Maury observed.

A few paces on they looked in on Genevieve to see her rocking backwards and forwards in a chair, her long hair matted, tangled and neglected. She was moaning softly to herself and making those strange repetitive gestures over and over again with her hands.

"She wants to see her children," explained Gadret.

Maury looked at Gadret in surprise, Gadret catching the look explained, "I learned to sign when I was younger. There were disabled kids in my father's church youth club and I used to help out..."

Outside Maury's office Sanchez awaited their arrival, he stood up from his chair and shook their hands warmly in greeting.

"Thanks for giving up your time to help us out again Professor, we really do appreciate it," Maury opened the door as he spoke and ushered both Sanchez and Gadret inside.

Sanchez's map still dominated the table with its multi-coloured pins indicating the pattern of occurrences that he attributed over the years to 'la Bête'. Sanchez removed his jacket and surveyed the chart, over the top of his pince-nez, as he hung it over the back of a chair, "Shall I begin?" he asked.

"Certainly Professor," invited Maury.

Gadret picked-up a large yellow envelope from Maury's In-tray and waved it at the inspector. "That will be the preliminary forensics report from Espadrels, " said Maury, "Open it," he directed.

Sanchez meanwhile began removing green-headed pins from the map, those that indicated livestock attacks over the past year that could be attributed to either the escaped wolves or the Soula-Boussé family. Their aim was identify 'hot spots' upon which any search for the family's dispersed camps could be made.

Large white-headed pins marked attacks and disappearances upon people. Gadret who was poring over the forensics data reached for a fibre-tipped marker and began scribbling on one of the pins: FS 26/8,

"Fabienne Sonnester," he explained, moving on to the one right next to it, "Fausto Claudi." He marked two more white pins, one for Alain Descartes on the blue of the Lac du Boucher and another in woods north-east of Mende for Enrik Rrukaj. There were seven pins remaining. "The report says that the remains of two unidentified victims were discovered in the midden."

That left five...

The door suddenly opened and the commissioner led Maury's old friend Pierre, the Inspector General, into the office, "Please carry on, don't mind us," said the commissioner. The two senior officers crossed to Maury's well-worn sofa and began quietly conferring.

As if aware, that the visitors had an ulterior motive Maury, Gadret and Sanchez moved their own business swiftly along.

"What else shall we remove Professor?" asked Maury.

Sanchez pondered for a few moments, "Actually, the more data we have the easier it will be to extrapolate and interpolate to predict likely locations." So saying, the professor pulled a small, expensive-looking digital camera from his pocket, "I'll take a photograph and go from there."

Gadret was still studying the minutiae of the forensics report.

"Do you fancy another trip out to Espradels sergeant," Maury asked him, "We still need to find out what Estoup's involvement in this case is. He'll need to be formally interviewed, so I suggest you take Lalande along with you."

The professor soon took his leave, with Gadret offering to drop him home and presently Maury was alone with his visitors.

The commissioner spoke first, with Pierre sitting back watching Maury's reaction, "Well done Maury, your team has done an excellent job. Your own performance has not gone un-noticed...", Pierre gave Maury a conspiring nod, "Which brings me to the real business of our visit.

"As you know, your attachment to the gendarmerie here in Mende has never been properly formalised, and although your speciality is homicide investigation you have been used wherever I have found it expedient..."

The commissioner raised his eyebrows, as if expecting Maury to protest, but Maury was just wondering as his superior spoke whether he was going to be promoted or sacked.

"We're in a bit of a pickle financially, I can't afford to squander the talents of a ranking detective on such relatively minor duties as Missing Persons, and our homicide rate is too low to justify employing a full-time homicide specialist..." the commissioner paused, as if unsure what to say next, but he was saved by Pierre's interruption.

The Inspector General sat forward and took over, "On the other hand, my area of command is beginning to struggle, we have had a major population influx over the past few years and we find ourselves short of experienced manpower."

"Are you offering me a job Pierre?" pressed Maury, determined to see the two politicians come to the point.

Pierre sat back and laughed, "Yes, I am. I need an experienced detective to lead the Homicide and Major Crime Department in Narbonne. You'd have to also liaise on a peripatetic basis with the offices in Beziers, Carcassonne and Perpignan."

Maury could scarcely believe his ears, he was being offered a future he had always thought to be a pipe-dream. Accept and he would be living and working in the region that had always been his spiritual home, or refuse and effectively see himself out of a job.

"I'd like to speak with my wife first," said Maury. Pierre and the commissioner both nodded, looking pleased. "When could I give you a definite answer?" he asked.

"We could chat this evening, Marie-France invited both Jeanette and I to dinner," said Pierre, rising to his feet, "It will be nice for us all to get together again, Jeanette is very excited."

* * *

All was calm and quiet at the Soula farm, the cattle softly lowing as they pulled at the fronds of fresh hay he had provided. The yard was bathed in warm welcoming sunlight, the only ominous distraction was the flapping yellow tape that the police had left around the house to demarcate it as crime scene.

Would he live here or in his old place when the farm came his way, he wondered? Soula's was a little smaller than his own house, but it had large verandas and no nearby neighbours, it sat in splendid south-facing isolation. The soil was good here too, he'd plant a kitchen garden by knocking down the tin lean-to Soula had used to garage his jeep and reclaim the land.

He wondered what state-of-repair the house's interior was in, and ignoring the cordon, ducked under it and climbed the steps to the front door. The key was in its usual place under the flower-pot and he turned it in the lock and entered a tile-floored kitchen with a wood-fired range, a large oak dining table and a dresser. This led into a small, comfortable sitting-room with an ancient television that served as a shelf for displaying family photographs rather than viewing, a threadbare Persian rug on the rough wooden floor and la pièce de résistance, a brand-new wood-burner sitting in the grate.

Yes, thought Estoup, given the choice, I'd live here.

He climbed the rickety staircase to the first floor, and followed a small corridor that led into a light and airy dormer bedroom, the bed made and unused, with views of the wooded mountainsides. Back along the corridor he found a larger bedroom dominated by a large unmade double-bed and a dark wardrobe. This room was en-suite with a functional white-tiled bathroom with WC and a large enamel bath full of dirty water. He rolled his sleeve up and plunged his arm into the bath to remove the plug, but as his flesh contacted the water his heart skipped a beat – it was still warm.

Estoup realised that this probably meant that he was not alone on the property. He un-crooked his shotgun and 'closed it up' ready for action then carefully retraced his steps through the house looking for evidence of habitation. He found none and was soon back on the veranda overlooking the farmyard. Nothing appeared out of place, so he relocked the front door and returned the key to its hiding-place. He decided against a tour of the barns and outbuildings, let whoever was watching him see him peacefully depart. He stepped into the yard.

A sudden blow to the side of his head sent him reeling and falling to the floor, the rock that had felled him clattered over the cobbles and as his head span he became aware of a figure detaching itself from the shadows of an outhouse.

* * *

Pierre made his apologies and left to see to other business with agencies in Mende, leaving the commissioner with Maury. They were overlooking the map.

"Then this," said the commissioner, sweeping his hand over the map as if to encompass it, "is largely solved.

"Forensics can run a test to determine if there are any DNA matches for any persons on our missing list against the evidence we recovered. Once Gadret has ascertained what Estoup's involvement is with the

167

case, if any, your investigation is largely concluded. After all, the main suspect is dead, his accomplices our secure in our cells and because of their mental health and disabilities will be sent to secure institutions for the rest of their lives without any need for committal to the judicial system. That's a bonus, because it would be hard for a prosecution to stick with so little evidence.

"But you need to know that once you've tidied those ends your work here is done. I cannot afford the manpower or resources needed to search for those dispersed camps that could be out there *somewhere...*

"After that, there is nothing keeping you here any longer Maury." These last words were said in a kindly manner, but they had a finality that hurt, "You've got a week."

"Anyway," said his superior, "You need to confer with your wife."

Maury did not argue, Marie-France had to faced, "Yes Sir," he said.

* * *

Gadret and Lalande pulled up outside Estoup's house in Espradels. As usual the village was deserted except for the two lost looking dogs sulking on Estoup's doorstep.

Knocking on the door raised no reply so the gendarmes split up and looked around the barns and outbuildings of the farm, before returning empty-handed to the car.

"Maybe he's up at the Soula place," suggested Lalande, "He was up there yesterday seeing to the animals."

Gadret nodded and they got back into the car and turned it around under the mournful gaze of the mongrels.

* * *

Maury had sensed that his life was on the brink of change before today's bombshells. It was a wake-up call for him, now he would have face Marie-France to discuss what to do with their stale marriage.

It was crunch time, and he knew that if she refused to leave Lozère with him, he would leave alone and begin another life. But also deep within were stubborn vestiges of their first love, that in times of crisis had been his succour.

He entered the house to find Marie-France singing girlishly to herself as she rolled pastry on a cold marble slab. Hair had escaped from her bun and she had white flour marks on her face where she'd used her fingers to tame the wayward strands. She looked up at him as he entered, a proud smile crossing her face when she saw how resplendent her husband was in the suit she had chosen.

"We need to talk," said Maury, "There have been some developments at work."

"Okay," she smiled, "Let me finish what I'm doing. Read the mail while you're waiting."

Maury removed his jacket and hung it over the back of a dining chair and reached for the large pile of papers. There was just one plain official-looking envelope sitting atop, what appeared to be, a pile of junk mail. The watermark identified it as a communiqué from the bank. But, to his surprise the junk mail was in fact a pile of brochures from estate agents in the Narbonne area.

He looked up at his wife who was studying him, "Bureau Narbonnais," she said, "Third page, second property down."

It was the top brochure, he opened the page she indicated and found the property she identified; a Mas in the Corbières, just twenty kilometres south of Narbonne. The beautifully proportioned old farmhouse with its gently sloping Spanish-tiled roof was shaded by Cedars of Lebanon, the place was reasonably priced but subject to offer.

Without wiping her hands, Marie-France crossed from the table and sat in his lap giggling as she held his cheeks in her floury fingers and looked him in the face with suddenly young and laughing eyes. "You'd better like it," she said mischievously, "It's ours!"

Maury said nothing, he melted as they kissed and he wept.

She kissed his wet cheeks in concern, "I'm sorry darling. I knew about your transfer weeks ago from Jeanette, but I couldn't say anything until Pierre made it official. You know Jeanette, she helped me sort out selling this place to buy the Mas. I had to break into our savings to do it...Please don't be angry."

Maury held Marie-France tight to him and his lips caressed her ear, "I'm not angry, I'm glad." he whispered.

\* \* \*

It was Gadret who found Estoup.

The old man was hanging by his neck from a rope passed over a beam in Soula's barn. The top of his hatless head was curiously bright in the gloom, as his body swung slightly a few centimetres above the littered remains of a dismantled shotgun.

That his death was inflicted by another was obvious, the rope which passed over the beam was knotted to the front axle of an ancient tractor in the corner. There was blood trickling down across his face from an angry impact wound on his temple and fresh blood dripping from wounds to his chest that had torn through his shirt.

The knife that had inflicted these was lying next to the gun, a large old Opinel, probably Soula's own. As his eyes accustomed to the low light levels Gadret could see that the wounds in the old farmer's chest spelled out a four-letter word: BETE.

A shadow darkened the doorway and Lalande entered, looking at Estoup he simply muttered, "Merde!"

\* \* \*

When Gadret tried to reach Maury, he found the number unavailable, so he rang Control in Mende, who redirected his call to the next person in his chain of command – the commissioner.

Gadret told his superior about Estoup's murder and its strange circumstances.

"Damn it Gadret! I was hoping we could put this whole sorry case to bed..." said the commissioner in frustration, "Sorry sergeant, this isn't your fault, how are you going to proceed?"

"With your permission I'd like the forensics team and some gendarmes to conduct house-to-house enquires to join me and Lalande."

The commissioner gave Gadret what he wanted, then sat silently considering his options.

Reluctantly, the commissioner pressed the telephone button for an outside line and dialled Maury's home number.

* * *

So, thought Gadret, that's why the commissioner and the Inspector General had been there to see Maury this morning. They must have thought that the case was closed – finding Estoup murdered was a wholly unexpected development.

When they arrived, Gadret deployed his gendarmes, sending them to work in pairs on house-to-house enquiries within the area of Espradels and its outlying farms, he also send a pair to reconnoitre the chaos.

He had Lalande once again assist the forensics men at the crime scene. The forensics men were quick to conclude that Estoup had indeed been murdered and the event had occurred just minutes before his body was discovered.

As for Gadret himself. He chose to visit la Répetille, an isolated farm which bordered the Soula farm.

* * *

La Répetille sat alone in an island of green fields surrounded on all sides by deep forest.

Alighting from the car, Gadret was astonished by the absolute silence

171

of the place, except for the occasional caw of a wheeling crow and the soft burble of the rill he crossed to approach the house, the place seemed to absorb sound. The hairs on the back of his neck rose as he was reminded of Orlazabal's forest clearing.

The house itself was a typical single-storey building of the region, with thick stone walls, small shuttered windows and a red-tiled roof.

As he approached to knock upon the front door a voice challenged him, "If you're the police, I've nothing to say!"

It was an old woman's voice coming from the side of the house, he followed its sound to find open French doors and a wizened old lady sat knitting in a rocking chair. "Madame Chabalier?" Gadret asked.

"I told you, if you're the police I've got nothing to say."

"There's been an incident in Espadrels. I wonder if I could ask you a few quick questions?"

"What sort of incident this time? All those blue lights flashing on the mountain last night, has it got anything to do with that?"

"Someone's been killed."

"Ah! Soula was a good sort, I won't say a word against him...Go on, be off! I told you I've got nothing to say."

"No, it's not Monsieur Soula."

"Not Soula? Come closer young man, so I can see you,"

Gadret stepped forward as directed so she could see him, "You're not from round here." she said, as if disappointed.

"I'm from the gendarmerie in Mende," Gadret explained.

She shook her grey head, her needles clicked, as if tutting, and she continued knitting, "You're not from round here," she repeated.

"No," Gadret conceded, "I'm from Charente."

"Never been there," the old lady stated, falling silent again. "So who has been killed then?" she asked suddenly.

"A man called Estoup."

Madame Chabalier, stopped knitting, leaned back in her chair and let it rock a couple of times, "Can't say I'm surprised, he's had it coming that one," she said.

The old woman's venomous tone surprised Gadret, she seemed almost happy that the old man had met his death. "What makes you say that?" he asked.

The old woman put her knitting onto her lap and looked at Gadret with rheumy, yet intense, hazel eyes, "Because of what he did to that poor boy of Soula's..."

She continued looking at him, as if expecting Gadret to recognise what she was talking about.

"You mean Hercules?" asked Gadret when the old lady came out of a sort of reverie and picked up her knitting.

"Yes, Soula's boy Hercules. Estoup had him working up at his farm now and again for pocket money. But it turned out he was buggering the boy in the stables. Course, the boy's a backward mute, so he must've thought he'd get away with it. But he got caught fair and square!"

"Who by, Soula?"

"No, no, Soula knew nothing, he didn't know 'til later why his boy was trying to kill himself. No, it was Boussé came across them. But Boussé was Estoup's business partner and he told the boy to go home and then tried to cover it all up. But they forgot, they did, that the boy was an elective mute – he eventually told someone..."

"He told his father?"

"Oh no, he never spoke two words to his father in his life. There was only ever one person the boy would ever talk to apart from his mother – God rest her soul."

173

"Genevieve?"

"Yes, he'd chit-chat non-stop with her about everything. They was really made for one another those two. He told her when she came back from that there fancy school in Alés on holiday. She went mad she did, and she never forgave her father for keeping it quiet and especially for not telling the boy's poor father what Estoup had done to his son...It caused quite a rift, I can tell you, she hated her family from that point on."

"Did she tell Soula?"

"Genevieve's not really mute, she's embarrassed by the way she speaks. She's got a cleft palate, you know, and it sounds like she's snorting when she tries to speak. But, when you get to know her and listen carefully you can tell what she's saying."

"What happened when Soula found out?"

"Nothing much, he went to the village waving his shotgun around and refused to do any business with either Boussé or Estoup and told both of them he'd shoot them, if they ever went near his boy or his land again. Then, I'm told he sent the boy off to Provence to farm with a relative."

Madame Chabalier fell quiet, shaking her head in disgust as her fingers deftly worked the wool and needles.

"You seem to known the Soula's pretty well," observed Gadret.

"Soula was my first cousin."

Gadret felt a pang of guilt for being the one to have killed a man who seemed, misguidedly or not, to have only been protecting his family.

"Have you seen or heard anything strange today? Have you seen a strange car or someone you don't know or normally wouldn't see?" he asked, getting back to the business that had brought him to la Répetille.

"No. The only car I've seen today is yours."

"Anything or anyone strange then?"

"Well, there was all that stuff going on up the mountain last night."

Gadret looked at his watch and made a quick calculation, "No, this would be sometime this afternoon."

The old lady shook her head, her mouth suddenly tight-lipped, "Only stranger I've seen in the last few days is you," she muttered.

Gadret felt that Madame Chabalier knew a lot more than she was letting on. He tried a less direct approach in order to tease out some of this information, "Have you heard about what was going on the mountain, Madame?" he asked.

The old lady shrugged, "They say on the radio that the police found Hercules and Genevieve and that they have got something to do with that German girl's disappearance."

Gadret nodded, "That's right. I was there."

The ancient eyes lit up, "Were you?"

The Sergeant lowered his voice to a conspiring whisper, "I can't say too much, it's an on-going investigation."

Madame Chabalier, went straight to the most shocking revelation, "Is it true that they became cannibals to survive?" she asked.

Gadret nodded, "It seems so." As he spoke, the sergeant's fingertips worked on his mobile phone's keyboard and sent a text to Maury.

* * *

Maury's mobile vibrated to indicate receipt of Gadret's text, he stopped laying the table and pulled it from his pocket to read it.

Marie-France entering the dining room with a large case of flowers for the table, saw her husband's jaw set as he read, "Work?" she asked.

"Yes," Maury replied but smiled at his wife in reassurance, "But it's something I can deal with from here." Marie-France looked pleased.

Maury dialled the Gendarmerie and asked for the custodial sergeant, "I want Hercules Soula and Genevieve Boussé put in the same cell and I want them to be recorded."

"But, they are mutes, sir!" the custodian protested.

"Please, just do it."

* * *

"Bloody hell! Sarge!" said the junior custody officer calling over the custody sergeant, "Listen to this."

A voice was tumbling words like a torrent, rushed, breathless and excited. The overseer looked into the cell through the one-way glass, Hercules was laying on the floor with his head on the crouching Genevieve's lap talking to her. She kept shushing him and for a few moments he'd be quiet and then start again.

The custody sergeant had not imagined the big man's voice to be so high, "Are we recording this?" he asked.

* * *

Hand-in-hand they watched the sun set over the lake, then walked back to their open fire. Yves resurrected it with some dry tinder and Jess admired his handsome profile as the flames cast their golden glow. He returned to sit at her side, carefully pulling a soft fleece blanket over her shoulders as the temperature fell and the first stars began twinkling in the cloudless sky.

Suddenly Jess shivered, Yves, concern in his voice, asked if she was cold. "No," she replied, "I think someone just walked over my grave."

She looked about her, at the yellow glow from caravan windows and listened to the quiet murmurings of families eating together on terraces or under awnings and felt her spirit quieten. But the utter depth of the darkness under the trees that bordered the site somehow still emanated menace.

She was being silly, she thought. Everyone's been talking about cannibals since the news broadcast this morning, before that it had been 'la Bête', and now she wished they'd holidayed elsewhere.

She pulled her boyfriend closer and looked into the dancing flames of the fire.

* * *

When Gadret returned to the gendarmerie it was obvious from his gendarme's reports that their house-to-house enquiries around Espradels had drawn a blank. No-one had seen anything or anyone of any interest and no-one seemed to grieve, apart from the man's dogs, over Estoup's sudden and violent demise.

The ever-dependable Lalande had contacted a contractor to take over looking after both farm's livestock.

The autopsy report shed no new light on the circumstances of Estoup's murder, he'd been knocked senseless by the blow to his head, dragged into the barn then strung up to choke to death. The letters were carved into his chest post-mortem. There were fingerprints galore but no matches, the perpetrator was an 'unknown'.

However, Madame Chabalier's revelation about Hercules' propensity to talk in Genevieve's company had struck gold. The custody sergeant had recorded two full hours of communication between the two before once again separating them.

Now Gadret sat with headphones and a notebook, rewinding, slowing and repeating the garble until he could make out a few key points in Hercules' monologue and note them.

*W*hen rumour of its fantastic feats crossed the Channel, Englishmen, safely sheltered in their island, poked fun at the terrors occurring in Gevaudan.

*A London broadsheet wrote satirically that a French army of 120,000 men had been defeated by a fierce animal and that after eating 25,000 cavalrymen and a whole artillery unit, had itself been defeated by a female cat whose kittens it had mistakenly eaten.*

*It was all too much: the honour of the country was at stake and Louis XV, normally indecisive, knew he had to act. He ordered the royal gun-bearer, Sir Antoine de Bauterne to go immediately to Gevaudan and bring him the mortal remains of the monster.*

*Antoine, his son, his servants, his guards, his valets and his bloodhounds arrived in Gevaudan and his first act was to dismiss d'Enneval, then he conscripted men to carry his luggage and care for his dogs. He acted all high-and-mighty, as if he were already the all-conquering hero. Dismissing this pomposity the Beast challenged him, appearing in a nearby meadow as de Bauterne took his midday meal, and made off with an old woman, Marguerite Oustalier, and left her dead after ripping the skin clean off her face.*

*Antoine seemed unperturbed, he organized a few fruitless scouting expeditions. Peasants said he looked impressive but was no more able than his predecessors.*

*Surprisingly, after three months of trial, error and failure Antoine left, with his entourage, for a part of Auvergne where the Beast had never been reported. He went to the wood of the abbey of Chazes where wolves were numerous. He lay in wait until he saw a large animal, with a gaping mouth and bloodshot eyes. No doubt about it; it was the Beast! Antoine shot, the Beast fell, a bullet in its right eye, it got up again and de Beauterne's second bullet caught it right in its body; down it tumbled, dead.*

*Antoine and his guards dashed forward: the dead Beast weighed 100 pounds, was nearly six feet long, and had enormous teeth and huge feet. It was a large wolf, quite ordinary except for its size, and it was carried in triumph to Saugues where the surgeon Boulanger performed a post-mortem examination.*

*Seven or eight children who some had seen the Beast alive were summoned and they declared, under pressure, that they recognized it as the Beast. This success was officially minuted and a certain Mr de Ballainvilliers, a toadying local official, wrote His Majesty an enthusiastic letter in which he thanked Him for saving the people of Gevaudan.*

*The Beast's corpse was quickly dispatched to a taxidermist in Clermont, stuffed and sent to Fontainebleau where the King laughed at the credulity of peasants whose superstition had transformed an ordinary wolf into an apocalyptic beast.*

*Because he saved the kingdom from this nightmare, Antoine was decorated and received a pension of one thousand pounds. His son made a fortune by exhibiting the Beast in Paris; ten years later, it was still shown in country fairs. La Bête du Gevaudan was officially dead and forgotten.*

*The same could not be said for Gevaudan. The incredulous people could not believe that their king could have been taken in by such a hoaxer. Yes, Mr Antoine had killed a beast but it was not **the** Beast.*

*They readied themselves for the next onslaught.*

September 5

They'd missed one. The one that had killed Estoup, the one who had thrown their rifles into the midden, the one who had laid out Thomas' body after death and made a funeral pyre of the lair in the chaos. They'd missed a child.

Those hand movements of Genevieve's - sign language - she'd pat down on the head of an imaginary child with each of her hands, calling for her *children*. A supplication, not for her dead, but for her living ones.

They'd missed her. The daughter who washed and brushed her mother Genevieve's, hair.

Maury knew, they'd missed one.

\* \* \*

Jess woke up cold and pulled herself into Yves' warm body and reached for her sleeping bag with her hand. She succeeded in pulling Yves' cover from him, he grunted, and now they both lay naked on the air-mattress. She laid his cover over them both, it was pathetically small but it was intimate. As she dozed back off she was aware of birdsong in the half-light of early dawn and a flapping sound as the breeze rippled the canvas of the tent, it must be a loose guy line she thought, they'd see to it when they rose.

\* \* \*

They met early, summoned by pager, in Maury's office.

Gadret had passed on his notes to the inspector and he'd reached the same conclusion, somewhere on the mountain was the one who got away, a cannibal killer, a young cannibal killer – and her name was Théa. They had no physical description, but she had to be a teenager, strong enough to string up a grown man, though admittedly Estoup was little more than skin and bone.

The dog teams would start in Soula's farmyard and barn and attempt to find a scent they could track, they carried military-grade radio gear and automatic weapons. On a hunch, Maury provided the fuel-covered wolf pelt they'd found on Estoup. "This may have her scent," he explained.

With the dog teams despatched Maury and Gadret turned once more to the large-scale map, "Which way will she go?" Maury asked aloud.

Gadret pointed to a concentration of pins north-east of Espradels, "According to Professor Sanchez, every other year the family used to rotate clockwise from Espradels during the seasons. South-west in the spring, then west, north-west and north in the summer. Normally, at this time of year they'd be somewhere in this area."

It seemed apt somehow to see that their quarry was heading back into of the upper reaches the valleys of the Allier and Loire, to the old hunting grounds of la Bête du Gevaudan and the site of the family's first known atrocity – le Lac du Boucher.

"We should alert our colleagues in le Puy, perhaps they can lend us manpower. And alert the gendarmerie in Langogne, circulate a bulletin and ask them to report anything suspicious," Maury directed.

* * *

To their handlers surprise the dogs soon found a scent using the wolf pelt. While one team were led to the village and Estoup's forlornly empty house, the other was led around the farmyard and eventually to the back door of Soula's equally empty property. By the back door they found a wet, soiled bath-towel and the dogs responded to this new scent by pulling their handlers up the mountainside. This team recalled the other, and before they continued together northward into the woods they contacted Mende with their updated status.

* * *

"She's heading north," said Gadret, replacing the receiver.

Maury grunted in acknowledgement and then rose from his chair,

"Let's head to the gendarmerie in Langogne, we will be closer to the action there."

* * *

The trail followed the contours of the hillsides, always in cover where possible, giving habitations a wide berth and using culverts to avoid crossing roads. It was a tortuous route but it consistently bore northward.

Once, the dogs startled a wild pig, sunbathing in a clearing with her striped piglets – they squealed and ran off into the under-brush noisily.

Stopping for a quick rest and some refreshment the handlers agreed that the girl's familiarity with the lay of the land was impressive.

* * *

Maury and Gadret entered the reception area of Langogne's gendarmerie to overhear two officers laughing with the desk sergeant,

"It's got to be a prank," said the sergeant.

"Well, no-one at the campsite is owning up to it," replied his colleague.

"Maybe you'd better have a chat with the Baptiste boys, they're practical jokers and they don't live so far away," suggested the sergeant.

"Yes, I suppose we could," said the junior officer still chuckling as he and his colleague wheeled away from the desk wishing the two plain-clothes men "Bonjour" as they passed.

"Has something funny happened sergeant?" asked Maury showing his I.D.

The man suddenly went serious and straightened up from his slouch over the counter, "Oh, just someone playing a practical joke on some campers - stole all their clothes and belongings during the night. They're probably hidden nearby."

"Where is this campsite?"

"At Naussac, by the lake," replied the desk sergeant, and then to his great astonishment the inspector asked for directions.

* * *

At the Camping de Sous-Bois du Lac the receptionist pointed out the location of the emplacement they were seeking on a large wall map.

They drove down a gentle slope toward the glittering Grand Lac de Naussac to a quiet area of the site set aside for tents. There they found a young couple, she black and he white, taking down a small tent, the trim figured girl came straight to address them when she saw their car's official registration plates, "Have you found our stuff already?"

Maury flashed his Warrant Card, "I'm Inspector Maury and this is my colleague Sergeant Gadret, we're detectives."

The girl's full-lipped mouth fell open and her eyes widened.

"I do believe two local officers are dealing with your complaint," Maury said reassuringly, "We're here on another matter. But would you both mind if we asked you a few questions?"

The girl shook her head of long blue-black ringlets and introduced herself, "I'd show you my Identity Card if it hadn't been stolen with our other stuff," she said sarcastically, "I'm Jessica and that's my boyfriend Yves." Yves lifted his chin in greeting when they looked towards him but he continued taking down the tent.

"Where are you from?"

"We're from Montpellier."

"Are you students?"

"No, we both work in Ikea."

"You're on holiday then?"

Jessica nodded, "We only got here yesterday."

"I'm sorry it's worked out like this," said Maury nodding toward Yves

183

now struggling to put the canvas into a tiny bag, "Are you going home?"

"Yeah," Jessica said with a sigh, "We've got no stuff now. We had planned on hiking..."

"Have you got a car?"

"No, my parents are coming to pick us up."

"That's a long drive," Maury paused as he saw Gadret press forward and then start helping the boy re-roll the tent, "Tell me Jessica..."

"Call me Jess."

"Okay Jess, can you tell me what happened."

"We woke up this morning and all our stuff had gone!"

"Everything?"

"Except for the tent, the air mattress and a single sleeping-bag, everything!"

"Clothes, shoes, food, equipment?"

Jess suddenly started giggling, "Yeah, we woke up naked wondering why we were so cold, then we saw the tent was open and all our stuff had gone. We had to shout to get a neighbour's attention. Lucky they always have a pile of spare clothes at the Reception, stuff people leave behind. This is not normally my colour you know!" she added in disgust looking down at her purple tracksuit, "The police were called straight-away and we made a full report to them."

"Indulge me Jess," said Maury warming to the girl, "Tell me as much as you can about what was taken." He pulled out his notebook and looked up to see that Gadret and Yves had managed to bag the tent.

They compared notes, standing together on the flattened grass where Jessica and Yves' tent has so recently stood. "Well, if it was Théa, she's got food, money and clothing to last," remarked Gadret.

"Oh, it was Théa all right," said Maury quite definitely, raising his finger to point at a group of men approaching with their dogs along the side of the lake.

As Maury predicted the dog teams came right to the emplacement, but the dogs soon started dragging their handlers north-west to skirt the south side of the lake; Maury and Gadret joined them. But the trail they were following suddenly veered toward the water and the dogs howled in frustration.

They were at the end of a small peninsula jutting into the lake, their quarry could have gone either straight ahead across a hundred metres of shallow lake or made shore-fall left or right of her point of entry into the water. The teams split up, while the detectives remained where they were. Soon word came from the team that went left that they'd located the trail again, it was still skirting the lake to its south side but making once more for the heavy cover of a pine forest.

They halted to allow the other team to catch up. One of the handlers, a local, pointed out the clock-tower of a village church, "That's Rocles. In the churchyard there's the grave of a little girl that was killed by the Bête du Gevaudan. They found her remains about here, where we're standing, but they never found one of her arms. Magdeliene Mauras she was called..."

"That's your surname," said his fellow handler.

"Yep. That's how I remembered."

When the other team re-joined them, they followed the dogs, passing by Rocles and then descending through thick woodland down to a torrent, where once again Théa appeared to enter the water.

The river ran south to north forcing the teams to waste more time trying to figure where she'd come out. After an hour both teams returned to the waiting detectives, "Merde!" exclaimed Maury when it became obvious that they'd lost the trail.

* * *

185

*They knew the police might come, after that fateful afternoon when the stillness was broken by ten loud gunshots coming from the track that ran from their grandfather's farm up to the base of the chaos. They'd emerged for their lair to find their grandfather's surreally propped body riddled by nine bullets and saw the jeep descending haphazardly back down the track, its driver slumped over the wheel. But their father would not leave, so sure was he that his father's killer was Estoup.*

*Foolishly, against Thomas' and her own advice and pleas, the family remained in the vicinity of Espradels to recuperate. But their little brother, Freddy, wandered off to get milk. Thomas was sent to find him, but the fell-runner had seen both brothers and she escaped and came back with a company of soldiers.*

*They were still preparing to leave when the gendarmes arrived at the foot of the chaos along the track they'd tried so desperately to conceal. She and Thomas had tracked them, hoping against hope, that they would not discover the lair so well-hidden in the jumble of stones. But it was a vain hope once the men had come across the midden and their stupid young brother again made an untimely appearance. So, she suggested sabotaging the vehicle they'd arrived in, to create a distraction, while they made good the family's escape.*

*She'd almost succeeded, as Thomas kept watch, in removing a fuel can and setting the car ablaze when the shot that hit Thomas rang out. She almost shouted out, as she saw him stumble and crawl away back towards the chaos rather than away from it.*

*Then, the rain had fallen and the men lost his trail and she'd watched hopefully as they looked to be about to leave, until the sound of her mother screaming, when a wounded Thomas reached the relative safety of the lair, made them turn back toward the midden and the back entrance to the cave.*

*She followed close enough to see them reach the ledge and the older, fatter one slope the rifles against the cave wall and when they entered* she climbed up and threw the vile things into the midden.

Then came the sickening sound of shooting from within, as she positioned herself to look over the lair's main entrance. She'd actually vomited in fear and anguish, fearing the worst until the policemen emerged escorting her parents and little brother. Where though was her twin?

She watched until they were gone and entered the cave to find her brother lying dead on the blood-soaked paillasse. She laid him out resplendent in the wolf-hood that he always claimed gave him special powers. But this time he had not been invisible, their bullets had found him and drilled through his beautifully deformed young body. So, she returned for the fuel-can, remembering her grandfather's cautions about leaving trails or evidence, and set the place on fire.

Once outside she wondered what to do, then she realised that there was more evidence to be rid of, the fuel-can itself and her own wolf-skin shroud, so she decided to bury them. She put them down while she went to find a digging implement and was shocked to find both items had disappeared when she returned. And then she'd seen that detestable creature, that beast, Estoup sneaking off with them just as the column of police vehicles arrived.

She wanted vengeance for her grandfather, her brother, her family, but most especially for her poor father Hercules. What better than to see that vile old paedophile pay for the crimes he'd committed on that poor tortured soul? That poor man who would talk non-stop to the females in the family of all his childhood hurts and of a curious love-story between him, his chosen one and the land of Lozère. So, she'd circled cautiously behind him as he lay watching the policemen from the edge of the forest.

But instinct had stayed her, just as she was about to pounce upon him form deep cover, and two armed men beat her to her family's mortal enemy. She saw him fall shot, then bundled away and then she watched the army of men on at work on the mountain until sleep found *her.*

*In the morning the men were gone.*

*What should she do now, bereft of her family? And then she remembered the contingency, "If anything should happen," said her grandfather as he taught her one of his many skills, "and you find yourself alone, you will need to get far away from here and make another life for yourself. You're resourceful and bright enough girl, to get by in the world – you can stay hidden by looking as if you belong."*

*So, she'd returned to the family farm to find it abandoned and she'd been enjoying the delicious indulgence of a bath, her first step toward joining civilisation, when she heard someone in the farmyard.*

*Théa got out of the bath carefully, drying the soles of her feet and wrapping a towel about herself she went to a window that oversaw the yard. Looking out she saw Estoup, he was seeing to the animals, already acting like he was Lord of the Manor.*

*Grandfather had always maintained that the man had designs on the farm, here he was acting the good neighbour, now that he could trespass on the property without being blasted by Soula's shotgun.*

*When he went between the sheds she quickly made her way downstairs, grabbing her clothes as she passed through the landing and had just managed to close the back door behind her when she heard the keys turning in the front.*

*She was changing into her clothes outside the back door when she heard Estoup's footsteps in the kitchen. She risked discovery if she loitered, so she dropped the towel and ran into the deep shadow between two outbuildings and waited.*

*Her right hand found a loose stone in the wall against which she desperately pressed to remain invisible. It was just the weapon she needed. When Estoup, at last came out of the house she struck quickly, while he concentrated on descending the steps, she launched the stone, seeing it strike the old man's temple. As he fell stunned, she ran* forward quickly and took his shotgun, patted him down and found his Opinel knife and laid both weapons behind her. The adrenalin coursing through her gave her strength and a strange clarity.

She dragged the moaning and dazed Estoup to the same barn in which her father had once tried to take his own life after this pathetic creature had abused him. She knew there was a rope, used to haul bales onto the first floor, she dropped Estoup to the floor and found it, threw its heavy end over the beam and tied a noose around the old man's neck. He attempted to wriggle free, but his movements were still clumsy and uncoordinated so she sat him up, taking up the slack in the rope by looping its other end around the front axle of her grandfather's broken-down tractor. Holding the rope tight, so that the old man's neck was stretched, she stood in front of him, "Please stand up Monsieur Estoup," she asked calmly. But the old farmer seemed not to hear, his hands went to his neck to loosen the noose, his eyes looking but not seeing her, so she pulled on the rope and he was forced to stand or choke. When he was on his feet she pulled some more to keep his neck stretched and he teetered there on tiptoe.

"Please," he said, "Let me go." His eyes, wide and wild, at last set upon her and he seemed terrified to see that his tormentor was a girl.

"No. You must pay for what you did to our family."

"Your family? What family?"

"Soula."

Estoup went suddenly still, "Soula?"

"Yes, Soula," Théa repeated calmly, "You did bad things to my father."

"Your father? Who is your father?"

"Surely you must remember a simple, mute boy called Hercules?"

She didn't wait for his reply, she pulled on the rope so that he was suspended a few centimetres above the dusty floor secured it with a knot to the tractor axle and, without pity or remorse, watched him kick,

189

*spit, twitch and then, finally, die.*

*The world should know what sort of man this was, she thought as she recovered the Opinel and shotgun from the yard. She broke the shotgun down and strewed the bits under the slowly spinning corpse, then opened the Opinel and carved deliberately into the dead man's chest with its blade.*

*This time they will bring dogs, she thought returning to the house to recover her clothes and her own long-bladed knife. She pressed on as quickly as possible towards Langogne, never rushing and always on guard, following the familiar contours that led toward the Grand Lac de Naussac where she had seen people camping. Tents gave little security, all she needed to do is watch the campers carefully and identify which ones were likely to have what she needed, then under cover of darkness steal those things away.*

*Théa reached the edge of the Camping de Sous-Bois du Lac as the sun was setting and she watched the young couple walk from the lakeside to sit beside their open fire. He was tall and white, she medium height, slim and black, they looked happy, they were ideal.*

*She catnapped until the campsite lay sleeping. The glowing embers of the fire gave her an ideal reference point to find the couple's tent. She heard the girl talking in her sleep and her boyfriend's soft regular breathing. The front zip opened noiselessly and she reached inside, her fingers found a heavy rucksack, then a pair of lightweight walking boots and a neatly folded set of clothes. Reaching further in she recovered a handbag, another set of clothes and a smaller pair of boots. Pleased with her haul she took it a few steps away, opened the rucksack and put the clothing inside it, then tied both pairs of boots by their laces to it. She hoist it upon her shoulders and put the handbag over her neck.*

*Now she had to slow down the dogs. She reached the lake and stepped straight into it, careful to keep her swag dry, first wading out and then wading along parallel to the shore before returning to dry land after*

190

*about fifty metres.*

*Next she had to lose them. She made her way through the woods past the village of Racles to a torrent, entered the river and then waded north, downstream. It was difficult going, the river-bed was rocky, the stones slippery with weed, but she needed to persist to lose the dogs. Where there were larger stones midstream, standing proud of the water, she removed her burden and laid it upon the rocks while she removed her clothing and buried it beneath stones on the riverbed. She put her knife in a pocket of the rucksack. She reached the junction with the larger and shallower river Clamouse, naked.*

*In the grey light of the false dawn she sat on an island at the river junction and opened the rucksack. She pulled out the clothing, carefully examined each item and made two piles, one to keep, the other to discard. Inside she also found food and eagerly fell upon an energy bar relishing the rare taste of sugar. The smaller boots, to her complete surprise, were a good fit when worn without socks, the larger pair were consigned to the discard pile. She wondered if the girls' sports bras would fit, and tried one over her breasts, it felt constricting and strange but she kept them nevertheless. She put the items from the keep pile into the rucksack and then looked through the handbag. Money would definitely be useful, but little else interested her, except a large hairbrush and a pair of sunglasses; these items were stowed in a pocket of the rucksack.*

*Taking the discards and the handbag she re-entered the river, still naked, and followed it downstream, heading north, until she found a beach. She carefully hid the items in a hole in the riverbank, walked over the sand making footprints and then carefully erased most of them. She looked at her handiwork, now her pursuers would assume she was continuing north, the hidden items should fool them into thinking she was covering her tracks.*

*In reality, she intended continuing south, upstream along the course of the Clamouse. She returned to the rucksack, hoist it upon her shoulders and continued for several kilometres. In a bend of the river she found a ledge formed when the river was in flood, it was shielded from view by the branches of a submerged tree and would make a good temporary camp, she pulled the rucksack and herself upon it.*

\* \* \*

Acting on a hunch, Maury suggested they keep pressing north following the river downstream, but reaching the junction where it met with the Clamouse put them in another quandary.

Again, one team went north while the other went south and Maury and Gadret waited.

Soon they heard the dogs baying downstream and they followed the noise until they reached a beach, a handler held out the handbag and the other items for the detectives to see, "She tried to hide them, but you can't fool dogs so easily!" he said.

His partner pointed at the other evidence, "She tried to erase her footprints but she missed a bit of one over here." He pointed at the partial print of a heel-press, then downriver, "She's still going north." The dog teams left in that direction.

Maury and Gadret decided, their feet sore from walking, to return to their car in Naussac.

\* \* \*

Théa found it impossible to sleep, could she hear the far-off bay of dogs? Her mind whirled and she wondered how everything had gone so wrong?

Now she was alone; a few days ago she had her family.

Today her grandfather was dead, Thomas was dead, her mother, father and little brother were probably imprisoned.

She had no remorse over killing Estoup, it simply had to be done. But other deaths, unnecessary deaths, could have been avoided. To kill for food or survival was one thing, killing for the sake of killing was

192

another.

*She knew her parents had resorted to cannibalism almost from the outset, but they'd had rules, golden rules, that had protected them against discovery for over a decade and a half. The eating of human flesh became an option only when there was no other prey and their survival depended on it. The victim had to be adult, a person alone in an isolated place. No property of the victim's was to be touched or taken. The victim should be killed quickly, calmly, efficiently, the body butchered and the unwanted parts disposed of in a place where their discovery was impossible.*

*But, when Hercules became weakened by illness, Thomas demanded the role of provider. His apprenticeship went well, under his father's guidance he had tracked, killed, butchered and disposed of the solitary fisherman on the banks of the Lac du Boucher.*

*But the next killing went wrong, Thomas seemed to have such a hunger for human meat that he started ignoring the rules.*

*She was with him then, it was lucky she was, for he attacked a forester who was in the company of his workmate. The man detached himself from his friend to answer the call of nature when her brother attacked him, but he botched the coup-de-grâce from the blade that was supposed to enter the man's neck and pierce his heart. Instead the wounded man fought back and shouted to his companion for help, and his friend came with two other men. She could see them clearly standing on the ridge above Thomas as he began stabbing wildly into the man's chest with one hand and clamping his mouth shut with the other. She could not believe that the men could not see the fountain of blood or hear the thrashing legs below them. So, she'd had to think quickly. She was carrying the fur of the wolf that Thomas trapped, she pulled it over herself and crashed noisily through the undergrowth to distract them. Seeing her, the men had screamed and run away. When she heard engines start and the squeal of tyres on gravel she knew the ruse had worked.*

*But, the episode seemed to have elated Thomas, who blood-spattered and standing over a corpse that had half its usable meat ruined, took the wolf-skin from her and wore it as a cape and began laughing and dancing in ecstasy. It was as if he'd been intoxicated by causing terror.*

*Later, events in the ravine with the young couple, revealed another side of her brother that she had not so far seen and it was to prove much more strange and frightening.*

*She and Thomas were returning from a three-day hunting trip, each dressed in their wolf skin costumes, his sourced from a wolf that had succumbed to wounds inflicted by the bullets of an angry farmer's rifle, to one of the family's network of seasonal lairs. Their route took them near a ravine. The hunt had been poor, they had found prey enough for themselves, but they needed surplus to feed the family. In the ravine they spied the ideal prey, a solitary fisherman, headphones on his ears, sitting on the spray-damped bank.*

*They were moving in to prepare an ambush when the man suddenly started packing his things away. They were out of position, but Thomas was confident that he could be taken before he reached the road some kilometres away, so they followed gradually closing the gap. However, the man suddenly stopped and hid himself behind a tree.*

*This strange behaviour was confusing. But when they heard the soft murmur of voices they understood that there were people somewhere ahead. Thomas sent Théa left while he went right although she protested that their planned attack should be aborted.*

*"I want to know what he's looking at," explained Thomas.*

*So, she flanked left and found herself with a view of a pea-green tent. The voices were coming from out of sight, on the other side of the fragile structure, there was no sign of movement, so she withdrew, returning to her original jumping-off point.*

*The man was still there secreted behind his tree looking into the camp, but of her brother, there was no sign. So she went right, as he had*

194

done and found him hiding in the undergrowth looking from this vantage point into the camp and at the man looking furtively, like them, at its occupants.

The man was clearly staring at a naked young blonde woman, sitting on a spread-out blanket reading a book. Théa noticed that her brother was equally transfixed. The woman's skin was golden brown, her body well-developed, with heavy white breasts, and Théa realised to these two voyeurs she was an object of desire.

"We should go," Théa whispered to her brother.

But her brother would not come, he remained where he was even when she withdrew into deeper cover. Even when the fisherman moved on, Thomas remained watching.

Théa was torn between loyalty to her brother and adherence to her family's unspoken code. This was a first, never before had they remained so long in the close proximity to people. They risked discovery and there could be no end gain, there was no viable prey. How many people were in the cam, at least two, maybe more? They were to take human prey in isolation, this was too near the road. Thomas was once again putting them both in peril.

But, should she leave him to it?

If he is caught, will they find the rest of us?

Who knew that we were more than one? The driver of the car that had crashed when its headlamps lit them up as they were crossing the road the other night?

She had decided to leave, when Thomas came crawling back to meet her.

"They are moving down towards the ravine," he whispered in obvious excitement, she had never seen him so keyed. "There are two of them, a man and the girl. We could ambush them both."

"Both?" Théa asked.

*"We'll kill him for meat."*

*"What about the girl?"*

*Thomas said nothing, he just moved off. Théa hesitated, then followed her brother, with a rising sense of unease, toward the ravine.*

*The couple were easy to catch-up with. The man was standing on the pathway while the girl was sat at the base of a tree, having removed her footwear. Thomas must have seen this as his opportunity, roaring as he ran forward, brandishing his three-clawed hoe he fell upon the man, striking him on his upraised arms with its prongs, and kicked the screaming girl in the head. Thomas' hoe slashed for a second time, into the man's arms again as he desperately parried this second blow away from his face. The blonde rolled unconscious, her nose spurting blood, onto the path into Thomas' legs and this momentary distraction allowed the man to turn and run. Thomas turned to Théa who was running to his aid, "Get him!" he shouted.*

*She had little choice. By now the man was screaming and running wildly along the path, looking over his shoulder every now and again to see that she was in pursuit. Then, suddenly he lost his footing, bounced off the trunk of a tree with a sickening crunch and fell headlong from the narrow path, over the cliff, into the river below.*

*She looked over the edge but there was no sign of the man, so she found a place she could scale down the sheer rock and made her way along the river to find him. She found blood, stones, mud and fern fronds where he'd fallen, but no sign of his body. Théa knew she should find him, but when she heard a woman's screams she reluctantly retraced her route, rescaled the cliff and returned along the path. The screams were coming from above the path, so she climbed up and was shocked to find her brother raping the golden-skinned girl.*

*Unseen, feeling sick and full of dread, Théa returned to path and waited until the screams turned to sobs. Then she heard a thud and all went eerily quiet. Presently, Thomas emerged carrying the unconscious girl over a shoulder, his face a shiny self-satisfied mask. He saw his sister looking up at him from the path below. "Did you get him?" he asked.*

*The last thing she wanted at that moment was to have to interact with someone towards who she felt such disdain and revulsion, but they had to face the situation they were in.*

*"He fell into the ravine, but I think he's still alive," she said.*

*Thomas climbed down to her, there were scratches on his face where the girl had fought him. Théa hoped they hurt.*

*However, her brother seemed unconcerned about the events of the last few minutes. He looked over the edge of the ravine at the drop and the torrent below, "If he's alive he'll have to come this way. Stay here and wait. I'll see you back at home."*

*"What are you going to do with her?" Théa demanded, feeling pity for the girl, hoping that Thomas would bring her misery to a quick end.*

*"She's mine," replied Thomas walking away down the path.*

*The blonde girl dangled limp, her clothing torn and soiled with blood and earth, her pretty face now a swollen mass of welts and bruising, swinging as her brother carried her away.*

*Then, waiting concealed, with a view of the ravine, for either the man to appear or darkness to fall, Théa knew that she could not live this life. This was the life her parents had chosen because of their circumstances. She did not know how she would do it, but she would get away somehow.*

Right now, as she lay on the ledge above the Clamouse with her head on a rucksack, she felt the same determination to be the captain of her own ship, to steer her own destiny.

Right now she needed help drawing up some sort of plan. Josephine Chabalier, her grandfather's cousin lived not so far away, she was wise and caring, perhaps she could be her mentor...

Théa knew that she would not sleep, she ought to get going.

* * *

"I'm no expert, but I have a nasty feeling that this girl is leading us in a merry dance," confessed Maury, as he and Gadret trudged back towards Rocles from the river, "I reckon she's doubled back and going south."

Gadret suddenly stopped and pulled his notebook from his pocket.

"What is it?" asked the inspector turning to watch the sergeant leaf through the pages.

"Madame Chabalier," Gadret muttered, "How the hell did she know so much about the Soulas? Who had she been talking with?"

"I thought you said they were related?"

Gadret nodded, "Yes, they are cousins, she said."

"Maybe you're right. After all who would you turn to in a time of crisis?"

Gadret looked up, dawning comprehension on his face, "Family!"

"So, maybe you have a point."

"We could call for back-up and have the place staked out in case she returns there," suggested Gadret.

"I doubt the commissioner would be thrilled at spending a load more money on a hunt for a feral teenager."

"But, she's a killer!" Gadret exclaimed.

Maury patted his belly, in the past few days he's lost weight, "We could forego lunch and do it ourselves," Maury suggested.

"I've got sandwiches in the car," Gadret said, with a chuckle, "Besides, la Répetille is on our way back to Mende."

"We've got about six hours of daylight.  It will probably take her two to three hours to get there." said Maury making a rough estimation in his head.

"We'll be cutting it fine."

"Ah!" said Maury, touching the side of his nose in a conspiring gesture, "Then, we'll have our friends from Langogne pick us up in the village here and get us back to our car."

They were on station at la Répetille within ninety minutes, they parked the car in a farm gateway, out of sight and found a vantage point from where to see both the house and its approaches. As good as his word, Gadret had sandwiches and a flask of hot coffee, so they ate as they took it in turns to watch the place with high-powered binoculars.

* * *

Crossing the N88 took more time than she'd anticipated, the main road, between Mende and Langogne was being used as a deviation and it was far busier than usual. She could not yet risk being seen and this was the first time that she had ever tried to cross a main road in daylight. At this rate she'd be reaching at Madame Chabalier's late in the afternoon.

* * *

Gadret shook the dozing Maury awake. "There's a girl crossing the meadow from the west, she's heading for the house," he said, passing the Inspector the glasses.

Maury focussed on the figure walking purposefully toward la Répetille, a brown haired teenaged girl in shorts and a man's shirt, wearing sunglasses and carrying a bag. "We'll let her enter, then we'll approach the house from its blind side. I'll take the front door, you take the back." said the inspector.

"Okay," said Gadret pulling his pistol from its shoulder holster.

Seeing the girl met by an old lady at the doorway Maury did the same, he nodded and together the men ran, crouched, towards the house. They went their separate ways when they reached it.   Maury found the front door ajar and he entered, shouting a warning, "This is the police! Stay where you are, drop any weapons and put your hands on your head! I am armed, resist arrest and I may shoot you!"

He burst into the living room where a shocked old lady was helping the girl into a hand-knitted cardigan, "Get out of my house immediately!" she demanded, "You have no right to be here!"

Gadret came into the room from some French windows, his pistol at the ready and trained it on the dumbfounded girl, who stood quaking, looking down its snub-nosed barrel. "You again," snarled the old lady at Gadret, "Have you nothing better to do than terrorise the neighbourhood? You had better have a warrant, this is outrageous!"

"I'm sorry Madame," apologised Maury, "We are here in pursuit of a criminal, and this young lady fits her description."

The girl turned to the old lady, "But I haven't done anything Grandma!"

"Hush child," said the old lady, "They're making a big mistake."

Gadret addressed the girl, "Do you have ID?"

"In my bag." She pointed at a large shoulder bag on the hideous armchair, he'd sat in just the day before.

While Gadret trained his pistol on the girl and the old woman Maury stepped forward and took the bag. The girl began to protest, "Careful, there are eggs in there! My ID is in my purse."

Maury found the purse and within was the girl's ID. "Name: Patricia Chabalier, Age:14, Address: La Grange, Laubarnès, Cheylard-l'Eveque, 48048," he read aloud.

Madame Chabalier folded her arms across her ample chest, "Now get the hell out of my house!"

Maury held up his index finger to indicate that he had not finished, "I'm very sorry Patricia, could you please tell me what you're doing here?"

The girl gestured towards her knitwear, "Duh! My nan knitted me a cardigan and I've come to try it on."

Maury insisted, "Tell me, how did you get here?"

The girl pointed through the window, "I walked from my house, which is only about fifteen hundred metres away, in that direction."

"NOW get out of my house!" the old lady hissed.


"Merde!" said Gadret as he and Maury made their way across the fields to their car.

Maury looked at his watch, "There's still time enough to continue watching here for a while and get me back to have dinner with Madame Maury," he observed philosophically.

The sergeant looked sideways at the inspector, Maury was not the morose detective he once was, he seemed unconcerned by their embarrassing debacle at la Répetille.

He's probably demob-happy, Gadret concluded.

* * *

Théa saw the men crossing the fields from the house, she knew who they were from their gait; the older fat one and the young good-looking one. The policemen from the chaos. Going to Josephine's house was now out of the question.

Which way now? Her feet decided it; south.

What was she doing? She could not go south. It was as if her feet were conditioned to taking her back to the maquis between Espradels and Mont Lozére. She needed to go towards civilization, but it was an alien concept to seek the company of others when avoidance of them was so ingrained in her psyche.

Hadn't her grandfather said that to become invisible in the world of men she'd have to remain in full view, to assert her place in society?

So, that is what she intended to do, to act as if she belonged in a world that was wholly alien.

She did not fear having to adapt. Théa had witnessed the adaptation of the escaped wolves from kept captive beasts into lords of the wilderness, and she knew she could do the same.

*Marvejols sat at the extreme western end of the family's seasonal range, a motorway had effectively served as its delineator. The Wolf Park was situated just within those limits, and from their spring lair they'd heard the wolves howling, from their enclave, a plaintive song projected at the moon on starry nights. To Théa and Thomas it was a song that both mourned and celebrated the wilderness that surrounded them, but to which they could not belong.*

*She and her brother were struggling to find passage through windblown trees in the wake of a particularly violent storm. Passing just a few metres from where they were scrambling over and under fallen tree trunks and branches a snorting wild-eyed stag thundered past. In its wake came wolves at a fast lope, seemingly unhurried but travelling rapidly nonetheless.*

*Théa and Thomas stopped in their tracks, mesmerized by the cruel drama they were witnessing. The stag, its flanks foamed and steaming with sweat had run itself into a cul-de-sac. It roared and stamped in frustration as it found itself hemmed in by an impassable tangle of windblown trees on one side, a deep black bog on the other and the wolves nonchalantly closing the third side of an ever diminishing triangle. At bay, it lowered its mighty head and brandished its enormous antlers at its tormentors.*

*In comparison to this great beast the wolves were small, but what they lacked in size they made up for in tenacity. The largest approached the stag alone and attempted to circumvent its great horns, but the stag brought them down on the unfortunate wolf which yelped and withdrew shaking itself. But it was not deterred, after a few moments sizing up its formidable opponent it repeated its probing manoeuvre unsuccessfully time and again, until it withdrew fatigued.*

*Once this wolf had finished another took its place. The stag began to tire, its movements become more laboured and difficult as its slender hooves began sticking in the churned mud of the arena. A third wolf engaged with the great deer and received minor gore wounds for its trouble, and at this small victory the hart seemed to rally and draw strength, lifting it head proudly and staring at the watching wolves in defiance. But then the wolves came in pairs, then in fours, until finally all eight surrounded the exhausted stag and it succumbed to their persistence with a low resigned sigh. The largest wolf clamped its jaws over the large ungulate's nose and its life ebbed away. In victory, the wolves frolicked and howled a celebratory hymn to their transition from captivity to liberty.*

So, Théa turned west and when she reached a road she walked along it, as if she were a lost backpacker. Presently she heard the growl of a vehicle overtaking her and a white van slowly passed. A few metres ahead it stopped in the road. Apprehensively, she walked up to it to find the driver leaning towards the open passenger door window. "I can give you a lift as far as the turn off for Villesoule," he said, smiling.

The man was dressed in green overalls, in his twenties and he had a nice face, so she opened the door and climbed into a cab cluttered with old wrappers and cardboard cups. "Please, excuse the mess!" he said lifting a pile of documents from the seat and putting them on the floor., "Here let me take your bag."

He took the rucksack and put it on the seat between them. She sat and closed the door, expecting the vehicle to now move forward but it remained stationary, the driver looking at her expectantly. "Seat belt!" he said.

She nodded and put it on. With a cough and a cloud of blue smoke the van started moving.

The sensation was wonderful, Théa imagined it must be a little like flying, the countryside rushed by on either side as the van followed the grey asphalt ribbon. She put her arm out of the open window to direct the wind with her hand, the air rushed around her fingers and swirled into the cab to ruffle her hair. The tickling feel made her giggle in delight. The driver smiled and laughed with her, stealing occasional glances at his strange and pretty young passenger with the pale eyes, as he drove along through forests, sharp bends and hairpins.

They slowed at a village, turning left onto another road. Théa had lost all sense of direction, but she didn't care, absorbed in her first motoring experience. All too soon the driver pulled over and halted the van at a side road, "This is where I turn," said the driver. He pointed ahead, "The main road    is about one kilometre straight on."

She thanked the man, took her bag, alighted and watched the van move off. The man waved from the window and she lifted her arm and waved in reply.

Alone, she felt elated. She knew that she had passed some sort of test, the man had not looked at her in horror or fear, he'd accepted her, taken her at face value. Théa was not naïve enough to believe that this would always be so. But, if this was to be her new life she felt like she might enjoy it. She hoisted the rucksack onto her shoulders and made off in the direction the man had indicated.

* * *

Maury's phone vibrated, he answered it, acknowledged the call and replaced it in his pocket. Then rose to his feet and looked down at Gadret who still had the binoculars trained on la Répetille. "The dog teams have been pulled off and everyone is going home."

"Do you think we missed her?" asked the sergeant.

Maury shrugged, "I don't know."

Maury had been thinking about the girl, and that is what she was – a girl, that they were pursuing, about how things must be for her right now. She was alone in the world, separated from her family, probably frightened and desperate.

Yes, on the face of it she was a killer, she'd made a good job of despatching poor old Estoup. But by what moral code to she exist? Her family ate people for goodness sake! And what would anyone do if they came face to face with the abuser of a member of one's own family? One might not actually do the deed, but one would certainly want to. But Théa was proving to be resourceful and canny, giving fully-trained and equipped paramilitaries the slip. You had to admire that.

And while a part of him was wishing her good luck, another part was worrying that if she wasn't caught she'd go on killing people for food. And there was the rub – the policeman in him was saying that she needed to be caught quickly, while the father in him was saying "wait to see how it all pans out".

Now, at this present moment the trail was cold, so they had little choice other than to see if the girl would resurface. By then he'd probably be off the case and installed in his new job in Narbonne.

But, I am a policeman.

He was sure that at some time the girl would be coming back here, to her family, to the strangely over-hostile Josephine Chabalier who appeared to be awaiting her - the cousin to whom either Genevieve , or more likely, Théa talked.

Maury called the gendarmerie in Langogne, ordering his uniformed colleagues there to take over surveillance of the house at la Répetille. When they arrived, he briefed them, then he and Gadret left for Mende.

* * *

*Witnessing the wolves in all their savage glory had a profound effect on Thomas, so awed was he by them that he resolved to pit himself against them, he saw these new predators as competition.*

*Although her brother took pride in his natural athleticism, his fleetness of foot and his stamina were easily outdone by the wolves who could*

205

lope along all day at a pace he could barely match in a sprint. He declared one day that he aimed to trap one so he could examine one of these elusive creatures up close. He would use his one advantage over them, other than his ability to climb trees, he would use guile. He had to act quickly, before the wolves became wholly familiar with their new territory. He chose to use an old mine working as a 'trou de loup', a pit in which a wolf would fall if it could be tempted to take the decomposing hare he placed on its collapsible roof as bait.

He caught badgers and foxes, until at last a doleful howl came from the trap's location in the grey light of dawn, signalling that he'd at last been successful. Together he and Théa ran the eight hundred metres from their seasonal lair, to find seven grey wolves slinking around the top of the now-exposed pit. Seeing their arrival they reluctantly left their captured comrade and melted away into the trees.

Thomas had the idea to tame the captured wolf, like a dog. But when he attempted to approach even the edge of the pit the creature would bare its teeth, its eyes black and fixed, growl a warning, then fly up at him snarling and biting, its sharp white teeth snapping. When he attempted to prod it and strike it with a suitable stick, far from submitting to his attempted domination it would do its best to destroy this instrument of torture. He changed tack, the animal was quite obviously hungry, he threw little titbits into the pit, but the wolf barely examined his meat offerings, it caught his scent upon them and refused them. Over a few days this continued, the wolf was slowly weakening but its spirit was proving indomitable. Then one morning he arrived to find the wolf dead, Thomas climbed down into the pit to recover its body. It had not died of hunger, wounds to its throat indicated that another wolf, one able to scale or jump the pit's sheer sides, had come in the night to put it out of its misery.

Théa asked for the dead wolf's golden-grey pelt, its three insulating coats making it soft and warm to the touch. She scraped and tanned it, using it as a shawl and a close reminder of an animal that she'd come to deeply admire and respect, a fellow nomad in the remnants of an *untamed world.*

* * *

The deviation had slowed progress, the tachometer indicated that he had less than two hours driving allowed. Today was probably not going to be his day. The sun was setting, the clouds gilded by its orange rays deepening the contrast between light and shadow. He switched on the truck's headlamps as the road pushed through dark forests. The traffic had thinned, his red articulated truck was now seldom overtaken or slowed by other road users.

The large diesel engine began labouring the truck up the long slope in the shadow of the mountain, he had to work the gears to maintain momentum. The truck was almost down to a crawl. Then in the gloaming the lorry's lamps lit a pair of long shapely legs, an attractive bottom clad in khaki shorts, walking in the gutter as the col came in sight.

Maybe today will be my day after all, he thought, as he gave the hitch-hiker wide berth then lifted his foot from the accelerator to slow the already crawling lorry to a snail's pace. He looked in the mirror at the girl as he passed, she was tall and slim with long and shaggy chestnut curls, her breasts high but prominent, her slightly underdeveloped hips indicated youth, and most attractively, she moved in sinuous feline grace. At the col he pulled the truck into the side of the road and applied the handbrake with a loud hiss of compressed air.

His heart was racing, he told himself to relax, to follow his well-practiced routine in the few seconds he knew he had. So he readied the stun gun, switching it to 'on' and the zip ties and placed them within easy reach, behind his sun visor. Then he leaned over to unlock the passenger door letting it swing invitingly ajar. The girl had now reached the truck and was walking past the trailer wheels. He felt desire hardening and throbbing in his loins as she approached the cab. Then the door opened and the girl looked in at him with pale green,

207

yellow-flecked eyes.

Now was crunch time, he reigned in his mounting excitement and gave the girl a welcoming smile, "I can give you lift if you want mademoiselle, I'm going as far as Severac, if that will do?" He wanted her to accept the invitation, everyone knew there was a large service station with accommodation at Severac, it implied that he would be giving her a lift to somewhere safe. The girl's gaze was steady, she seemed to be assessing him.

* * *

Théa had seen that same look on the faces of the fisherman and her brother as they'd looked shamelessly at the blonde girl, naked at the entrance to the pea-green tent. She felt the driver's eyes on what he could see of her body, her cleavage, her breasts – it ignored her person, fixed only on her physical attributes – it was lust.

*When she reached the shelter of the lair she was disconcerted to find Thomas aggressively facing-off against their father Hercules who stood facing his far more physically intimidating son with their mother, Genevieve, at his side trying to reason with both. Behind her brother, in his corner of the cave, the girl lay unconscious.*

*Théa understood immediately what was going on, Thomas was defying his father by disregarding the rules, he was refusing to kill the girl. "She's mine," he was saying, "I need a mate. It's alright for you," he pointed at both his parents with a wagging finger, "You have each other."*

*Although angry at being defied, Théa could see that his reasoning had scored points, and his parents were already conceding defeat. The posturing continued for a few more seconds until Genevieve pulled Hercules away, "Let it be, he's becoming a man, this was bound to happen one day."*

*And so it was that the blonde girl had become her brother's chattel, she was kept naked in her brother's corner of the cave. Laying or sitting on* the skins that formed his bed, her hands fastened behind her back until he loosened her bonds to use her. This repeated cycle of rape, of little kindnesses offered, withheld and refused, of physical violence and degradation was supposed to break the girl to make her compliant to her brother's wishes. When the girl gradually gave up resisting him, or whispering a beseeching "Nien, bitte, nien,", or even her tears and crying, he thought she was submitting to his domination, to his vile display of misplaced machismo. Their parents thought it too. But, she was refusing food, letting herself waste away, preserving her spirit while she surrendered her body.

Her eyes would connect pleading with Théa's across the cave and Théa knew what she had to do. It is what a wolf had done for a fellow wolf. Yes, when the time comes I will help.

The time did come, a few days after their return to the cave the siblings went hunting. While Thomas went one way, Théa went another then doubled back to the lair. Hercules was languishing, still weak and sick in his bed, Genevieve was occupied with little Freddy who wanted his mother to play. So she crossed unchallenged to the blonde girl who watched her approach with steady, unfrightened, blue eyes. She pulled the girl to her feet and led her through to the back of the cave, to the ledge above the midden. There Théa used her knife to loosen the girl's bonds. The girl rubbed her wrists, stood there naked, lifting her face to the weak sunshine for a long moment, she shook her matted blonde locks and removed her little dolphin earring with its diamond eye and pressed it into Théa's left hand, then looked at Théa and nodded. For a moment Théa was paralysed, but then the girl took her right wrist and brought the hand and knifepoint up to her breast. Looking Théa imploringly in the eyes she whispered, "Bitte..."

When he returned empty-handed from his hunt, Thomas flew into a rage to find that his 'woman' had disappeared. He demanded to know where she was. Théa, her mouth full of meat got up to face him, still chewing, and offering up another morsel to her mouth, pointed to the family sat quietly dining and said, "We were hungry." His eyes widened

209

*and his mouth dropped open, a protest lodged in his throat. He threw off his wolf skin hood impotently, suddenly emasculated, and ran from the cave.*

She looked at the driver, she could emasculate him too, if necessary. His lorry was going in the right direction and being sat so high in its cab would be even more like flying! She climbed into the cab.

* * *

On the Col de la Pierre Plantée, they passed a big red articulated lorry pulled over on the side of the road with its hazard warning lights flashing. Maury recognised its familiar livery, this company's lorries were omnipresent on French roads. He wondered if it were experiencing mechanical problems, but when he looked back he saw that its passenger door was closing and it was remounting the shoulder of the tarmacadam. Its bright array of driving lights lit up the interior of their unmarked car as it followed down through the hairpins towards Laubert and Mende.

* * *

"My name's Guy," he lied, "Guy le Bilan." The girl barely acknowledged that he was speaking, she smiled then turned back to watch the skeletal forms of trees, whip past the windows. Stupid little bitch, you'll pay attention to me soon.

"I'm from Paris. Where are you from?" he lied again, wondering if she knew her regional accents. Obviously not. "Here," she replied, "Lozère," she added as an afterthought.

And here in Lozère is where you're going to stay, you stupid, stupid kid.

Okay, time for some fun, let's rattle your little cage. He made up another blatant invention, "I've got three kids, Huey, Dewey and Louie."

Her legs were great, toned, a bit scratched from hiking by the look of it,

210

they reached all the way up into that tight little...

"You are married?" she sounded shocked, disbelieving. He looked at her, and felt a little pissed off, the stupid little cow accepted his lies hook, line and sinker and then had the cheek to query the only truth he had so far told.

I'll forgive you, just this once because you have got great tits.

He went silent, driving steadily toward their rendezvous with destiny, trying to think of another game to play that would rack up the tension, give him a sense of power. They entered the outskirts of Mende, the car they had been following turned towards the town centre. They got stuck at some lights behind some kids in an ancient Citroen 2CV.

"I'm going to _uck you in the arse."

Now she'd notice him.

"Pardon?" she said.

"Aren't they nice old cars?"

He laughed to himself, yeah, you heard me right first time.

You'll start squirming soon and then you'll try to get out, but the door won't open and you'll try the seatbelt, but that's been fixed too.

The lights changed and he stole another glance at her as the green light lit her face. She didn't appear to be taking any notice of anything he was saying, she seemed fascinated by the old town around her.

\* \* \*

He was speaking French, but using words that she'd never before heard. She had not heard them from her poor impeded parents, neither her grandfather nor cousin. In fact, she was finding it hard to take everything in. Her senses were being overloaded with stimuli, the buildings, the lights, the fountains and sculptures, and the people – young, old, men, women all going about their business. Whatever the driver was saying, he seemed to be speaking for the sake of it. But, despite not understanding his words she understood that they had a dark undertone and so, unseen she slipped her knife from the rucksack pocket and put it under her thigh.

* * *

He was tiring of the game now, she seemed to either be deaf or she was as thick as two short planks. He'd bandied other filthy innuendo, getting increasingly coarse without any reaction. He fell silent and planned.

He thought of the road, running ahead in his mind, planning the route. In half-an-hour they'd filter south onto the A75 at Junction 39, they'd make better time on the motorway even though it climbed in steep ramps over the Causses, nineteen kilometres to Junction 41. Exit there and the old road would lead to the service station below Severac-le-Chateau. She would never suspect that somewhere on that old road they'd make an unscheduled stop, he'd conclude his business with her and he'd be able to make the service area without overdoing the hours on the tachometer.

Once its wheels hit the smooth surface of the motorway, the constant tone of the governed engine seemed to lull the girl to sleep. She put her head against the bulkhead and closed her eyes.

Little traffic, few witnesses to see the giant red truck slow for the exit at Junction 41 and turn onto the little-used departmental road. Two kilometres further and he made a left turn over the motorway through thick pines into a disused quarry. He'd made deliveries here when it was operational, it was horseshoe shaped with sheer limestone walls and a narrow entrance that the lorry effectively blocked. There he stopped, letting the engine idle.

Still the girl did not stir. He reached for the stun gun and the zip-ties keeping a weather eye on the sleeping beauty. Carefully, stealthily, he opened the driver's door and slipped from his seat to the ground, crossed in front of the cab and unlocked the passenger door.

Now he had to move quickly. He pulled open the door, startling the girl but before she could react he used the stun gun on her leg to incapacitate her, she shuddered and shook as the high voltage coursed through her and she went limp. He reached up and pulled her head down by her hair and attached a zip-tie around her neck.

Her hair smelled earthy, as he gripped her under the arms to pull her from the cab. His hand cupped her firm breast briefly. She was heavier than she looked, all toned muscle, he almost salivated with anticipation.

Something fell from the cab and clattered on the rough ground when he freed her legs – the bitch had a knife! He'd have a use for that when she came round. But first he needed to get her to the picnic table that was lit by the truck's headlights.

* * *

Théa felt her ankles dragging across the ground and hands under her armpits pulling her backwards away from bright lights and the sensation of something tight around her neck.

She reacted immediately, punching backward into the man's groin. He instantly fell backwards and she fell on top of him, twisting onto her right side and bringing her elbow down on his larynx. The driver gasped for breath and instinctively let her go. Free of his grip, she rolled away from him, got onto all-fours and tried to orient herself, there seemed nowhere to hide but in the surrounding darkness.

* * *

His groin hurt, her punch had instantly deflated his arousal. Worse though, was the pain from his bruised Adam's apple. Seething, in both humiliation and anger, he sat up to see her running away into the dark.

No-one had fought back at him before, usually the girls behaved like rabbits in headlights, they'd lay there sobbing while he used them. Then plead pathetically for mercy as he pulled on the zip-tie to shut them up, once and for all.

213

She really was a stupid bitch, she couldn't scale the limestone walls of the quarry and she couldn't pass the truck. She was trapped.

He slowly got to his feet, recovering the stun gun and gingerly made his way back to the lorry. He picked up the knife he could see still laying by the nearside front wheel, then climbed up into the driver's seat and switched on the array of spotlights, they flooded the quarry in harsh white light. There she was, it was pathetic, she was right there at the foot of the cliff staring in his direction. Just standing there waiting.

I'll be there in a bit darling, and I'll give you a good seeing to!

He switched on the interior lights, he needed to find the crossbow he'd stashed under the bed in the sleeper compartment...

But then she started moving, was she dancing on the spot?

No. He could scarcely believe it, she was taking her clothes off. She pulled her t-shirt off over her head exposing her torso and breasts, folded the garment and lay it down carefully. She was giving him a striptease to delay the inevitable. Good girl, carry on!

Then she undid the top button, unzipped the fly and pulled her khaki shorts down over her hips, her thighs, her knees and stepped out of them. She did the same with her panties, stepping free, exposing the soft furred v of her sex. She arranged the clothes nicely, deliberately. Walking boots first, t-shirt, shorts and panties. Then she straightened up, her right arm swung and something detached itself from her hand and sailed towards the windscreen.

He couldn't help himself, he instinctively ducked in the driver's seat and covered his face in his hands. With a pop, the stone struck the windscreen sending a crazy white spider web of cracks around a dark impact point right in line with the drivers field of vision. Pop! another well-aimed stone hit the windscreen, this time dead centre and then pop! A third so that the windscreen was an opaque mess.

Quick, get that bloody crossbow now! He found it, but found it hard to use the cocking aid in the confines of the cab, but with a little determination and brute force it was cocked and he loaded a bolt. He held it in front of him sweeping it from side to side to increase the field of fire as he got out of the cab. But, the girl was nowhere to be seen, he strained his eyes but she had disappeared.

Too late, he realised there was only one place she could be, the stones had been launched to cover her charge in under the lorry. Hands grabbed his ankles and pulled, he fell forward onto the crossbow which went off, driving the bolt through the bottom of his chin into his top front teeth and his nose. The pain was instant and debilitating, he could only lay there breathless as the girl used his own zip-ties to secure his hands and feet.

* * *

It wasn't some weird ritual to remove her clothes, she just didn't want them ruined. Besides, she knew that he'd fixate on her as she unclothed and that would buy her time. As she folded the clothes and stacked them neatly she was also secreting well-weighted stones into her hands.

The last thing he'd expect is her full-frontal assault and even as she launched the first stone she was up and running towards the truck, transferring the other stones in turn from left hand to right to be launched in sequence as she rapidly closed the gap. Then she slid in under the cab, feeling the heat from the still hot engine on her back as she waited for his feet to appear.

The injury inflicted by the driver's own crossbow bolt had been an unexpected advantage, otherwise she was planning to pop his eyes with her sharp fingernails. Now he lay face-down in the dirt, moaning from a bloody mouth and secured by the tough plastic straps.

She took her time, recovered her knife from the cab and cut the tie-wrap from her own neck with care. She remained deliberately naked as she helped the truck-driver up and made him hop over to the concrete picnic bench, she had some carving to do and she didn't want blood on her nice new clothes.

215

* * *

She knew that she had to leave the vicinity as quickly as possible, to put as much distance as possible between herself and the quarry under cover of night. She could not escape cross-country, she was now far away from familiar territory and landmarks, so she had to follow the road. Reaching the departmental road from the quarry's access track, she looked left and right not knowing which way to take.

She suddenly felt a wave of despair and loneliness crash over her. The stark reality of her situation, after the elation of the day's vehicle rides and the adrenalin-fuelled actions of the past half-hour, made her too desperate to care. She simply ran along the ribbon of road that was revealed by the weak light of a moon scudding along behind with her behind high curtains of wispy cloud. She hid at the approach of headlamps and made towards a glowing of the sky.

But the glowing did not signify approaching dawn, she was approaching a neon-lit limestone village. High on a hill above it brooding ruins looked as if they may offer shelter. So, carefully skirting the brightest lit of the village streets Théa found a well-worn pathway which led to a crumbled castle.

S ure enough the Beast showed up again.

In early winter, it took a girl in Marcillac and made a second meal of a woman from Sulianges whose two hands were the only things it spared...

Resuming its wanderings the Beast was again seen every day. There was no doubt that this was the same monster, it followed the same pattern as previously, taking a child or woman daily.

At night it entered villages, laid its claws on windowsills and looked in on kitchens.

It was not a wolf: the people of Gevaudan knew wolves, for in the past two years, one hundred and fifty two wolves had been killed in the region and the peasants could not be mistaken.

There were more tragedies: two little girls were playing in front of their house in Lèbre, when the Beast came and pounced on one and took her in its fangs. The other girl jumped on the Beast's back, held on tightly and was taken away. As she shouted for help, the villagers rushed to her aid... too late: the head of the child was ripped off, the face of the other destroyed.

The Gevaudan again begged for help; but its pleas went unanswered. Versailles had closed the case, acknowledgement of the Beast's continued survival was tantamount to questioning the good authority of the King or at least insinuating that he had been cheated. Which sycophant would dare to irritate the King for the lives of a few peasants?

The Beast was dead, Sir Antoine had killed it, end of story.

Still the Beast was on the rampage.

September 6

The touch of a wet nose on her skin woke her. A voice admonished the little wire-haired terrier that was nuzzling its friendly muzzle against her face, "Harry, get back here!"

Théa snapped awake. The dog was being called in a language she couldn't understand by an old, very thin, very tanned woman from the back of a scruffy van, parked haphazardly among stinging-nettles. The little terrier ignored its master, snuggling close under Théa's fleece blanket, as if to share her warmth. The thin woman rolled her eyes and stepped out of the van that Théa could now see contained bedding and kitchen equipment. Théa caressed the little dog's whiskery face and softly tried to shoo him back towards the approaching woman who was saying in highly accented French, "I am sorry. He does not usually behave like this!"

* * *

Maury was awoken by the persistent ringing of the telephone, when they moved house he'd make sure they didn't put one in the bedroom, so he pulled back the covers and reached out for the receiver being careful not to disturb Marie-France who still lay peacefully sleeping with her head on his chest. The clock said eight, they'd laid in. "Maury speaking."

"Allo. Inspector Maury, this is Captain Balthazar in Rodez. I have been instructed to liaise with you on a case."

"Yes?"

"There has been an incident near Severac-le-Chateau to which the local gendarmerie has responded, but I'm afraid that because the incident has technically occurred in Lozère, I have been told that you have to take over the investigation."

"What sort of incident are we talking about?"

"I think it would be better if we met up at the scene. Give me your mobile contact number and I will supply you with co-ordinates."

"Okay, I'll be there as soon as I can."

Maury replaced the receiver, held Marie-France close and kissed the top of her head, enjoying the warm scent of her hair.

"Are you going?" she asked sleepily.

"Yes," he replied.

\* \* \*

Harry wandered, once more, over to the girl who was warming herself in the sunshine, sitting on the ledge of an arrow loop, brushing her long hair. Annette followed in her dog's paw-prints, "I think he likes you." The girl patted the little dog and looked up at Annette with startling pale eyes and smiled.

Annette trusted her dog's judgement, Harry was a great judge of character, if he liked this strange girl then she wouldn't argue. "Could I interest you in breakfast? I've more than enough," Annette asked and added, "It's full English."

The girls face furrowed in puzzlement, "English?"

"Yes, like me," explained Annette brightly, "Egg, bacon, toast, tomato, mushroom, beans, sausage, tea, coffee, orange juice..."

The girl laughed, "That sounds wonderful!"

"Come on then Harry!" ordered Annette to the little terrier who was looking up into the girl's face and wagging the stump of his docked tail, "and bring our new friend."

\* \* \*

Driving past the gendarmerie in Mende, Maury picked up Gadret and they drove south-west towards Severac-le-Chateau together. They found Junction 41 and turned onto the old departmental road that ran parallel to the motorway. Soon they saw dark blue minibuses and uniformed officers manning a roadblock to control access to a well-surfaced unmarked access road. Maury showed his credentials and the sentries manning the picket pulled back the barriers to let them pass. They drove up over the motorway via the single-track flyover and down into a little forest of stunted evergreen oaks until they pulled up at another cordon of police vehicles. As they emerged from their car they were met by a tall well-turned out captain who introduced himself as Balthazar, the liaison officer from Rodez, "The gendarmerie at Severac were the first responders, but they come under the Aveyron command. But, as you can see, we are now east of the A75 motorway and in the area of Lozère's command. Therefore, you are to formally lead the investigation and I am to place the gendarmes from Severac at your disposal."

Maury nodded in understanding. Balthazar continued, "Let me introduce you to Adjudant-Chef Richard, the ranking local officer here." He called over a tall man, with the red nose of an imbiber and a gloriously orange moustache, "He'll take you up to the crime scene."

Warrant officer Richard shook the two detectives' hands with a firm grip as they formally made each other's acquaintance and then led them through the cars. He pointed ahead at a large red articulated lorry, "We found this truck here at 5.30am. It was blocking the entranceway into the disused quarry which lies just beyond it. It was still running when my men found it, so they had to climb over it to gain access. We reversed it out of position to allow access into the quarry."

"This unit operates from le Puy, its operator is one Paul Guy, a French national, aged 32, married but separated for the last eight months. According to his controller he'd made a run to the company depot in Lyon yesterday morning and was returning to Rodez with a mixed load."

Maury recognised the familiar ubiquitous livery. He'd noticed a similar truck yesterday while returning to Mende. All this company's trucks were the same marque, with little to distinguish one from another except their registration plates. As they passed they saw that the windscreen had been shattered by three missile impacts. Richard pointed to the damage, "I'll explain how that happened later. My officers entered the quarry and found a man zip-tied to that picnic bench right ahead of us.. We identified him as Paul Guy the truck operator"

Looking ahead they could see a concrete picnic bench of the sort often provided by local authorities for use in communal areas. This one was blood-stained and already flies were buzzing busily around it. In a blood pool congealing beneath was something black. Richard stopped and pulled a digital camera from his webbing, "Here, see for yourselves." The pictures showed a man lying face up on the table. His hands and feet were attached to the benches by zip ties, "Was he still alive?" asked Maury. "Yes," said Richard, "He's been taken to hospital in Mende. That's the closest Urgences."

The next pictures showed close-ups. First of the man's face, horribly disfigured by the crossbow bolt that appeared to have made entry from the bottom of his chin, pierced his mouth just behind his front teeth to exit through the top palate and the torn left nostril of his nose, "He won't be talking to us anytime soon," Richard remarked. "There was one more wound, I did take pictures but you're better of seeing for yourselves," Richard pointed to the black thing in the puddle of blood and spoke matter-of-factly, "That's his scrotum."

"Merde!" exclaimed Maury.

Richard gestured back to the truck, "There's more to show you in the cab, if you two gentlemen climb in through the passenger side I'll get into the driver's seat." They did as the warrant officer directed, Maury sitting on the passenger's seat while Gadret looked into the cab from the access steps. Richard pointed to a device attached to the inside of the windscreen almost at its very top, "This haulage company reduces its insurance costs by having a camera fitted. It points straight ahead, and records everything that happens in front of the lorry. In the event of an accident the film can help apportion liability. The data is

221

recorded onto a memory stick here," he explained pointing down to the little device, sitting in a slot beside the tachograph. Richard switched on the truck's ignition, and a buzzer sounded, "I'll start the engine. That will stop the air-brake alarm from sounding." With that the large diesel engine clattered to life, quieting as it warmed. Then, with a button press Richard activated the Satellite Navigation screen, "We can output the video it recorded onto this."

The picture quality was very low, black and white and grainy and there was no sound. A watermark in its top corner gave GPS coordinates, time and date. Richard was playing back video taken late in the day before. The truck is climbing through mountain roads and slowing as it climbs. It passes a female figure walking along the verge, all that can be seen of her in the headlamps are her long legs. Then the truck slows even more and turns onto the verge to stop. The lorry is stopped for a couple of minutes, a car passes on the road and the lorry re-joins the carriageway.

So, this is the same truck, the one I saw yesterday, thought Maury, recognising the police car that he and Gadret had used the day before.

Richard fast forwarded. The truck enters Mende, exits Mende, joins the A75 then exits onto the departmental road and drive that leads to the quarry. It enters the quarry, headlamps lighting up the empty picnic bench. A few moments later, the top of a man's head can be seen as he passes the front of the lorry left to right. The screen buzzes with sudden interference. A few more moments pass and then the man can just be made out dragging an obviously unconscious girl, her face obscured by long dark hair, by her armpits towards the picnic bench. The girl appears to regain her senses and her reaction is immediate, the man goes down and she falls on top of him and runs off into the darkness, picking up a bundle of objects the man has dropped. The man sits up holding his groin and throat he picks up a pistol shaped object, then he gets up and walks unsteadily back towards the truck. A few moments later powerful lights flood the quarry, the girl is standing at the back of the quarry, the definition is poor her face overexposed, it is just a pale shape. She strips off her clothes, folds them neatly into pile then stands again. She throws a stone towards the truck and charges forward launching two more stones as she advances, then dives forward out of view. A few more moments pass then the girl is pushing the man toward the bench. She halts him and makes him sit on the table, then she pushes him down so he is face up upon it, then she seems to be talking to the man while she cuts the zip ties at his ankles, shifts the knife to her other hand and then attaches one ankle then the other to the table. The knife swaps hand again and the girl undoes his jeans and with a simple flick of the wrist castrates him. The man appears to lose consciousness, and the girl then cuts his wrist ties and reattaches them to the far end of the benches. The girl walks back towards the truck.

"The crossbow was down on the ground on by the left front wheel. We found this here in the cab," Richard, reached back and pulled out an evidence bag with what looked like a grey plastic pistol, "It's a stun gun." He reached back again and held up another evidence bag with two more memory sticks, "These were hidden in the sleeper cab. Normally, if a drive has been incident-free the stick is reformatted and used again. We thought they may be important if the driver had hidden them away. We were right."

He replaced the stick in the dashboard with one from the bag. It loaded and Richard played it back. The lorry is going down an urban boulevard in half-light, the watermark displays 06:15, there is little traffic. A woman is running along the pavement ahead of the truck. The truck slows, overtakes her and then stops. A glitch and the screen goes momentarily blank. "It's been edited, that's when he used the stun gun," Richard explained.

The truck approaches a warehouse and stops at some sliding doors. The driver opens the doors, drives into the warehouse, apparently disused, and halts in front of an old iron bedstead situated in the centre of the room. The driver crosses in front of the cab. He reappears, dragging an unconscious girl, dressed in running clothes, by the armpits to the bed...

The other stick played a similar video. A girl is overtaken at night in a quiet urban street. The truck goes to the same warehouse and the driver goes through the same routine...

"I know who they are," said Gadret, still feeling angry and sick at the deprivation he had just witnessed. "Bertillon in le Puy has these two on his caseload. The first was a jogger in le Puy, the second a young girl going to nightclub in Yssingeaux."

Richard pulled out his notebook and opened a page on which he'd noted the GPS coordinates that were displayed on the screen. He'd also noted the location of these coordinates. There were three – le Puy, Yssingeaux and Retournac. "Spot on!" he said.

"What's at Retournac?" asked Maury. "The warehouse," Richard replied.

* * *

It was strange sitting where the driver would normally sit, but Annette's van was English, so Théa sat over the centre of the road with Harry on her lap as the van spluttered southward. The sun was shining brightly through the windscreen so she had her stolen sunglasses on and the vortex of air from the open windows blew her hair around wildly. She had one hand on the dog's chest the other on the pile of tourist brochures. The upper one showed glossy pictures of the monument they would visit on their next stop, a Templar village and castle. She looked at Annette and smiled happily.

* * *

Under Bertillon's supervision the le Puy-based forensics team searched the disused warehouse at Retournac. Guy had not fully attempted to cover his tracks, perhaps because his visits there were mainly legitimate. The warehouse and its land belonged to his estranged wife's family, he rented it from them at a nominal rent, with a view to developing it as a regional distribution centre. It was also registered as an interim depot for his work operations, so his visits there with the lorry raised no eyebrows.

The iron bedstead and its soiled bedding provided much useful evidence, indicating it as the site of the sexual and physical abuse of a number of women. Of his victim's bodies nothing was immediately found. When a back exit from the warehouse was discovered, the team quickly located a newly poured concrete base built to serve as a chemical and hazardous substances store. Bertillon ordered the concrete broken-up and the site duly yielded the mortal remains of three young women, all bound and garrotted with plastic zip-ties. The police team were expecting the bodies of the teenaged night-clubber and the jogger. The third came as a surprise, more decomposed than the others, indicating that her death had come before the others, her DNA quickly identified her as a twenty-four year old prostitute reported missing from a motorway service area near Lyon some eleven months previously.

* * *

DNA traces matched with those from Soula's farm at Espradels proved that Théa was the girl on the video who'd reversed the situation with Paul Guy, the rapist-murderer.

Gadret had stills produced from the footage and used the best to produce a circular to be disseminated throughout the Languedoc and Midi-Pyrenees policing networks. The photo showed her head and shoulders, the head confidently perched on a long neck, her dark curls partially obscuring her even-featured face. Her description followed; Théa Boussé-Soula, aged 16-17, height approximately 178cm, weight approximately 57kg, Caucasian, dark hair. This person is likely to be armed and dangerous, sought in relation to homicide in the commune of Luc, Lozère and with kidnapping and torture in the commune of le Massegros, Lozère. "Do you want me to circulate this to the Press and public information bureau?" the sergeant asked. "I don't think so," Maury replied, "This picture could be of anyone, we'll keep it internal for now."

* * *

Bertillon phoned Maury and told him about his team's discoveries at the warehouse, "We want everything you've got that can nail him for what he did to those girls. I'm sorry if it buggers up your investigation, but we've got to put this bastard away!"

"I understand," said Maury, "You'll get everything you need."

"I also want that shit Guy, in custody here in le Puy. According to the hospital in Mende he could be moved by ambulance, only ours is tied up ferrying his victims to the morgue..."

"We have one in Mende. I'll make the arrangements lieutenant. You'll have Paul Guy and all the evidence we've collected here brought to you."

Maury called Gadret over, "I've got a job for you sergeant." He sent Gadret to Bertillon with the evidence recovered from the quarry scene, with orders to pick up an escort and Paul Guy from Mende en route. Now, without the sergeant looking over his shoulder at his modus operandi he could conveniently forget to send the local gendarmes off looking for the girl along every road that radiated from the quarry site. His heart wasn't here in Lozère any more, he simply felt as if he was being delayed on his road south.

* * *

Gadret mused as he drove. Paul Guy had got much more than he'd bargained for when he chose the wolf-girl as his next victim and she had shown him mercy that he didn't deserve. Still, without the organs that got his hormones raging he was incapacitated, stripped of his bestial appetite and his cravings of power.

Why do people kill? for food? for power? for revenge? for fun? to prevent suffering or to protect? The Boussé-Soulas had killed for food; Guy for power, the ultimate control over another, to project his will and feed his dark hunger. Théa had killed in revenge, not for herself, but upon her father's abuser. Perhaps she had killed for other reasons too, but Gadret doubted whether it was for power or fun.

That made him think about what he himself was doing. I don't actually kill, but I hunt. Why do I hunt? For power, revenge, fun, or to protect or prevent suffering? Who do I protect if I pursue Théa? To revenge myself upon her grandfather Soula, whose inflicted wounds still ache and stab into my side? No, the only reason I may legitimately hunt is to protect or prevent suffering. Maury, goes soon, I will have his job. There are missing persons files still sitting on the gendarmerie's files, a suffering family behind each sad story. There, upon these I should direct my attention, to rule nothing in, to rule nothing out.

* * *

A transporter arrived carrying a lorry tractor unit. Paul Guy's was detached from its trailer and replaced. While Guy's was loaded onto the transporter in its place, its replacement pulled the trailer away, to deliver the goods aboard that still required delivery. It was soon followed by the transporter taking Guy's tractor unit to Toulouse for specialist examination.

Richard's local gendarmes walked the quarry site one last time to ensure that no last bit of evidence had been missed. When they were satisfied a crew of sapeurs-pompiers hosed the picnic bench and its area down with their appliance's equipment. With the site now clearing of personnel and vehicles, the warrant officer turned to Maury, "What now sir?"

"I thought that with my sergeant gone, I could review what we've got with you?"

Richard nodded, "Be my guest, I'll have one of my officers run you back to Mende when you're ready."

* * *

Madame Richard had cooked a fine meal, then made her excuses, leaving Maury sat with her husband and a bottle of fine wine, at the kitchen table, to talk 'shop'. The warrant officer was already conversant with the celebrated case of the Cannibals of Lozère. But the additional detail of Estoup's murder and the subsequent manhunt for his killer were new to him. "So, your girl was responsible for this?" he asked, rotating a photo of Paul Guy's pale form spread-eagled over the picnic bench his jeans dark stained. Maury nodded.

Richard then looked at Gadret's circular, describing Théa, then back directly at Maury. "Well, she seems to be heading away from your jurisdiction into ours, or maybe even beyond," he observed, bristling his orange moustache, "But, let me be honest inspector, nobody's going to be looking too hard to find her!"

Maury held up his glass of red, "Santé!" he said.

Responding to the continued lamentations of the people, the marquis of Apcher, one of the lords of Gevaudan, organized one last beat. Among the company of hunters who responded to this call was one Jean Chastel. He was 60 years old, born at the turn of the century, in Darmes, near Besseyres-Sainte-Marie. He was a solid and religious man; well-regarded by the whole region for his honesty and good conduct.

Jean Chastel stationed himself in front of Sogne-d'Auvert, near Saugues. His shotgun was loaded with two consecrated bullets, said to be silver, and he was reading from his prayer book when he looked up to see the Beast, "the real one".

Calmly, he closed his rosary, put it in his pocket, removed his glasses, put them in a case and returned them to a pocket…

The Beast just stood there waiting. Chastel shouldered his weapon, aimed carefully and shot. The Beast continued standing eerily immobile but Chastel's dogs responded to their master's command and ran forward, knocked it down and began savaging it.

Its dead body was loaded onto a horse and carried to the castle of Besques. There it was examined and declared to be «the Beast». The monster was plainly not a wolf, its feet, its ears and the hugeness of its mouth were of unknown origin. In its stomach the shoulder of a young girl, that had been devoured two days before in Pébrac, was found.

Chastel's Beast was exhibited throughout Gevaudan before being consigned to a box for onward transfer to Versailles. There, it was hoped, some learned fellow could identify its true species; and the King would realise he had been duped by Sir Antoine.

Unfortunately, the trip took place in the full warmth of August, and the Beast was in such a state of putrefaction that it was buried before anyone dared to examine it. So it will never be known what type of animal the Beast of Gevaudan truly was.

Chastel was introduced to the King who made fun of him, but when he returned to Gevaudan, the paymaster-general granted him a reward of seventy-two pounds.

But Gevaudan itself proved grateful, Jean Chastel became a local hero. There, his name and the legend of the Beast lives on. But, in la Sogne-d'-Auvert where the beast met its end, locals complain that "the grass does not grow", it is red tinged and no animal will feed on this damned grass.

September 7

The beep signalled the arrival of an email.

Laura poured herself an espresso from the cafetière and returned to her desk. She didn't recognise the contact, an Italian email address, but it was marked high priority. Cautiously, she opened the attachment she thrilled at the email's content, scarcely believing her eyes, and her joyful whoop brought her colleagues running. They demanded to know what news had so delighted their boss. Laura paraphrased, "Our last missing wolf has been found living and well in Altare, Italy! Local rangers were tranquillizing local wolves to tag them with transmitters when they noticed her tattoos, which identified her as one of ours!"

The lone wolf had made it.

Printed in Great Britain
by Amazon.co.uk, Ltd.,
Marston Gate.